P9-CME-652

WITHDRAWN
LVC BISHOP LIBRARY

Also by Amelia Atwater-Rhodes

SNAKECHARM)

Amelia Atwater-Rhodes

Delacorte Press

Published by
Delacorte Press
an imprint of
Random House Children's Books
a division of Random House, Inc.
New York

Copyright © 2004 by Amelia Atwater-Rhodes

All rights reserved. No part of this book may be reproduced or transmitted in any form or by any means, electronic or mechanical, including photocopying, recording, or by any information storage and retrieval system, without the written permission of the publisher, except where permitted by law.

The trademark Delacorte Press is registered in the U.S. Patent and Trademark Office and in other countries.

Visit us on the Web! www.randomhouse.com/teens
Educators and librarians, for a variety of teaching tools, visit us at
www.randomhouse.com/teachers

Library of Congress Cataloging-in-Publication Data

Atwater-Rhodes, Amelia.
    Snakecharm / Amelia Atwater-Rhodes.
        p.   cm.
    Sequel to: Hawksong.
    Summary: The peace forged by the love between Zane and Danica,
leaders of the avian and serpiente realms that had been at war for generations,
is threatened by the arrival of Syfka, an ancient falcon who claims one of her
people is hidden in their midst.
    ISBN 0-385-73072-1 (trade)—ISBN 0-385-90199-2 (GLB)
    [1. Fantasy.]   I. Title.
    PZ7.A8925Sn 2004
    [Fic]—dc22

                                                              2003020709

The text of this book is set in 12-point Loire.

Printed in the United States of America

September 2004

10 9 8 7 6 5 4 3 2 1

BVG

Snakecharm
*is dedicated to friends old and new, near and far,
and to all those who love unconditionally.*

she
saerra' Ahnleh
Mehay'hena-ke-lalintoth'fmperaine'val'maeke'daivtra
a'rsh'thu'varl'jas'mak

*Also,
I give thanks to:
Kel, for all you have given me, taught me, and put up with.
Sebby, for the knowledge that one can always be young, and always be full of fire.
Jesse, for being . . . Jesse; for long nights with cherry Coke and conversations.
Karl, for caring, for laughing, and for daily miracles.
To Kyle, Coureton and Sean, for inspiration and last-minute help.*

Ke'ke
la-varl'teska-s
Kel-ke-a'la-gen'varl-raviheah'varl-ke'ke-o'la'rahvis
Sebby-ke-heah-amaen' sheni-hena'val'vehlar'Kaya
Jesse-ke-hena'hena
ke-cincanon'chenya-ke'ke-cherry Coke-ke'ke-ha
Karl-kevarl-jas'jeal-ke'ke-varl'nesera'cinca'lar
a'Kyle-a'Coureton-a'Sean
ke-kayla-ke'ke-falmay'shni'jacon

To tears, to compassion, and to love.
a'vehl-a'jas-a'toth

a'le-Ahnleh

THE SHAPE

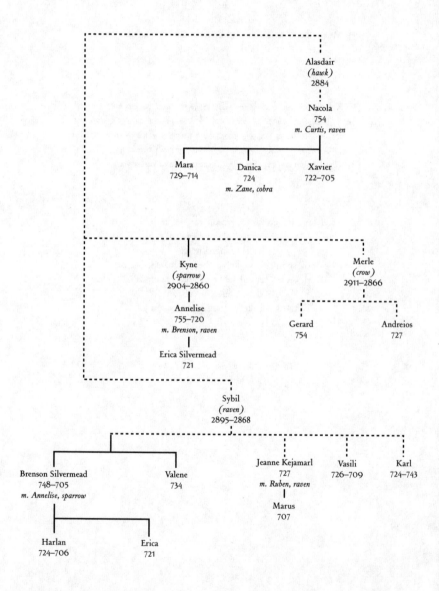

Alasdair
(*hawk*)
2884

Nacola
754
m. Curtis, raven

Mara
729–714

Danica
724
m. Zane, cobra

Xavier
722–705

Kyne
(*sparrow*)
2904–2860

Annelise
755–720
m. Brenson, raven

Erica Silvermead
721

Merle
(*crow*)
2911–2866

Gerard
754

Andreios
727

Sybil
(*raven*)
2895–2868

Brenson Silvermead
748–705
m. Annelise, sparrow

Valene
734

Jeanne Kejamarl
727
m. Ruben, raven

Marus
707

Vasili
726–709

Karl
724–743

Harlan
724–706

Erica
721

Dashed lines indicate not only a lapse of several generations, but also an indirect relation.

SHIFTERS

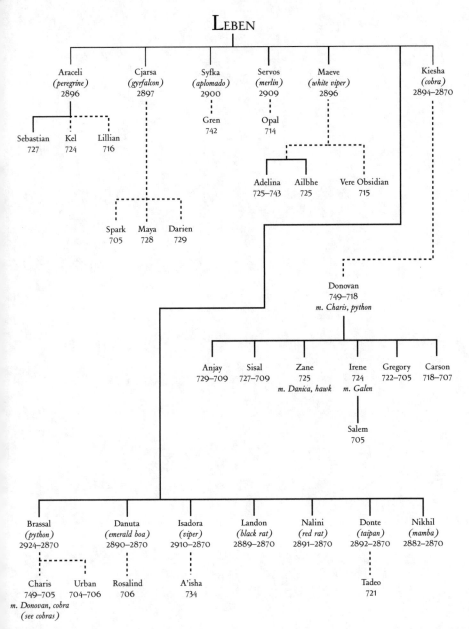

LEBEN

Araceli
(peregrine)
2896

Cjarsa
(gyrfalcon)
2897

Syfka
(aplomado)
2900

Servos
(merlin)
2909

Maeve
(white viper)
2896

Kiesha
(cobra)
2894–2870

Sebastian
727

Kel
724

Lillian
716

Gren
742

Opal
714

Adelina
725–743

Ailbhe
725

Vere Obsidian
715

Spark
705

Maya
728

Darien
729

Donovan
749–718
m. Charis, python

Anjay
729–709

Sisal
727–709

Zane
725
m. Danica, hawk

Irene
724
m. Galen

Gregory
722–705

Carson
718–707

Salem
705

Brassal
(python)
2924–2870

Danuta
(emerald boa)
2890–2870

Isadora
(viper)
2910–2870

Landon
(black rat)
2889–2870

Nalini
(red rat)
2891–2870

Donte
(taipan)
2892–2870

Nikhil
(mamba)
2882–2870

Charis
749–705
*m. Donovan, cobra
(see cobras)*

Urban
704–706

Rosalind
706

A'isha
734

Tadeo
721

PROLOGUE

WHEN EGYPT WAS YOUNG, and the first pyramids were being built with the sweat and blood of slavery, there lived a small civilization on the outskirts of society, led by a coven of thirteen men and women called the Dasi.

It is said that these thirteen were able to read the thoughts of mortals, and that they could bewitch any who looked upon them. When they danced their rituals together, they could summon the spirits of the dead, make the rain fall or cause illusions to rise from the sand.

Among their pantheon, they worshipped the dual powers Anhamirak and Ahnmik. Anhamirak granted life, light, love and all manner of beauty; her greatest gift to her people was free will. As all things must, she had an opposite. One prayed to Ahnmik for power, sleep and silent peace. He was not an evil god, but with power came force, and so while Anhamirak gave this world freedom and equality, Ahnmik's gifts included bondage and mastery.

Each side could not exist without the other, and so the speakers for this darker god stood as revered in the Dasi as Anhamirak's.

The twin powers were held in a precarious balance by the high priestess of the Dasi, Maeve.

As the story goes, a creature by the name of Leben appeared to Maeve. At first she thought he was a god, an incarnation of Anhamirak's son, Namid, and she bowed down to him. Then he ordered her coven to worship him alone—at which point Maeve realized that, for all his power, he was no god, for any true god would know that only chaos would follow if the balance was lost.

Knowing the danger he posed to her people if angered, but unwilling to surrender to his demands, Maeve seduced him, and in an attempt to win her favor, he gave her ageless beauty, and the second form of a viper with ivory scales. She insisted he do the same for all her people.

Leben gave the ebony scales and garnet eyes of a king cobra to Kiesha, high priestess of Anhamirak, and other graceful serpent forms to seven of her followers. The four whose worship fell to Ahnmik—Cjarsa, Araceli, Syfka and Servos—were given the majestic wings and deadly talons of falcons.

The magic Ahnmik had given the falcons, combined with Leben's gifts, was strong and dangerous, and soon they were driven from the clan for their reckless practice of it. Maeve's ivory-scaled kin were soon forced to follow, as the white vipers too fell to Ahnmik's lures and abandoned the balance they had once revered.

Reluctantly, Kiesha rose to power, and from her son—or so the story goes—the Cobriana line descended.

My own line. The line with garnet eyes and jet-black hair, which has led the serpents since the day Maeve fell to Ahnmik. We have ruled through famine, we have ruled through fortune, and for unknown generations, we have ruled through war.

Until now. I am the first of my line to rule through peace. These last few months with Danica have gone by so blissfully that I find myself doubting fate's sincerity.

Did Kiesha's kin feel this same queasy fear in the night, after Ahnmik's followers were driven away? Did those ancient serpents know their days were numbered by an enemy they had not yet even encountered?

According to avian myth, Queen Alasdair was given her hawk form after she prayed to the avians' sun god to lift her city from civil strife and poverty. She gathered her people and brought them peace and prosperity and turned a faltering city into a beautiful empire.

Avians and serpiente had never met before the day Kiesha was granted an audience with the new hawk queen. Neither had a reason to hate the other. Yet avian history books say Kiesha stabbed Alasdair in the back; ours say Alasdair's guards slaughtered the eight serpents in their beds. No one knows the truth anymore, only that the children of the slain retaliated swiftly, and years of bloodshed followed.

Ancient fears, ancient questions. Our war with the avians is over now. We do not know what hatred led to the murders of Kiesha and Alasdair, but I do know it is love that binds our realms together now. I thank the gods daily for the brilliant hawk who is my mate.

But older hatreds and ancient threats still remain. A missive reached us late last night: Syfka arrived at the Hawk's Keep yesterday, seeking Danica and me, and was told we were at the serpiente palace. The falcon is due to arrive here any time today.

During the war, the falcons supplied the avians with poison specifically designed to kill Kiesha's serpent kin—my people. Before the war, the falcons nearly destroyed the Dasi's civilization in their search for power and were exiled as a result.

The war is over.

What now?

Zane Cobriana
Diente

CHAPTER 1

A FLICKER OF SHADOW AGAINST THE SUN made everyone in the serpiente market pause in their business and look to the sky. The fluttering of wings and the sight of a diving sparrow chilled me.

Erica Silvermead, the sparrow who now shifted into her human form in front of me, had been guarding the front door of the palace. Her presence here meant that our dangerous visitor had arrived.

Politely excusing myself from the merchant I had been speaking with, I followed Erica into the palace.

Once we were alone, she confirmed my assumption. "Syfka, speaker for Empress Cjarsa, is at the gate. She has requested an audience with you and your pair bond."

I would have liked nothing more than to order the guard and the Royal Flight to ban Syfka from our lands, but insulting the falcons would be suicide. While the serpiente retained only ancient dances and half-remembered stories from the days of Maeve's coven, the falcons' powers were still strong. Their royal house supposedly consisted of the four

5

falcons who had once practiced among the Dasi, kept alive by a combination of Ahnmik's and Leben's magics.

If the legend was true, Syfka was one of those four and, as such, a creature whose might was too great to fathom. Even if it was false, Syfka represented an empire we could not risk slighting.

I nodded reluctantly, taking a detour to find my mate.

We caught Danica just as she was leaving the synkal, where her lessons were held. She was languid from exhaustion, but she smiled upon seeing me, and my heart warmed just from the sight of her golden hawk eyes lighting up. Then she saw my worried gaze, and her expression suddenly mirrored my own.

"Syfka is here?" she asked.

"At the gate."

Danica shuddered, but joined Erica and me on our hasty walk toward the entryway. "Syfka was never an enemy of my people during the war, but she made it clear that falcons held no respect for avians no matter how similar our second forms may seem. Whatever she is here for now, I suggest we deal with it quickly."

"We're in agreement, then."

Ailbhe, the head of the palace guard, was waiting with our visitor by the doorway. The white viper stood at strict attention, tension wavering in the air around his silent form, his gaze fixed not quite on the falcon, but never moving far from her.

Syfka radiated an aura of heat that rivaled even Danica's constant warmth. Her hair was pale gold, and in the front it faded to silver; her eyes were crystalline blue, set in milk-pale skin. Wings rose from her shoulders and cascaded down her back, with the golden undersides and brown, gray and black markings of an aplomado falcon.

She was stunning, and like all falcons, she had a magnetic air that could draw mortals to her like moths to fire—ultimately to meet with the same demise, if they dared offend her. Right now she was standing formally with her left hand clasping her right wrist behind her back. It was the respectful pose of a soldier, but Syfka's expression told me clearly that the respect was not for me.

As her eyes met mine, it was easy to believe this creature was as ancient as myth. She gave a nod that might have served as a bow, if it had been accompanied by anything other than obvious disdain. "Zane Cobriana, Danica Shardae, I appreciate that you are prompt. I am looking for one of our people, who I have reason to believe is in this area."

"A falcon?" I could not help frowning. "Not among the serpiente. Danica?"

My mate's expression remained calm, though I knew her well enough to feel her agitation and anxiety building. "You are the only falcon who has visited our lands in the last decade," she answered.

Syfka looked amused. "The falcon could have altered its form, its coloring," she explained, her voice patient, as if she was speaking to a young child. "I hesitate even to offer a gender, as that could feasibly be hidden, too. Unless you'd seen the person's falcon form, there would be no way to know."

"Then why ask us?" I replied, irritated by her patronizing tone only barely more than by her request. I struggled to keep my voice from revealing my annoyance. "If there's no way for us to tell whether someone is a falcon, how can we help you search?"

Syfka nodded toward Danica. "Though it seemed unlikely, I thought the criminal might have asked for asylum from the Tuuli Thea, since some on the island know of our past alliance with the avian people."

"May I ask what he or she has done?" Danica inquired.

"That is not your concern." Syfka's words were brisk.

I might have argued, had I thought the falcon was someone I knew, but I doubted that was the case. Someone trying to hide was unlikely to befriend the king of the land.

Danica also held back any protests she had. If we discovered the so-called criminal, we might dispute Syfka's words, but for now we might as well work with her.

Danica echoed my thoughts. "So many people pass through the court every day that a newcomer could remain unnoticed for some time unless he introduced himself to the Tuuli Thea. I can, however, see if my guards have noticed anything unusual."

"I will speak with the serpiente," I added. "If there are any newcomers in these lands, the dancers at least will know of them." While the Cobriana were the heart of the serpiente, the dancers were its blood; nothing went on in the royal house, the market or the most distant serpiente lands that the dancers did not know about eventually.

Syfka nodded curtly. "See that you do. I want this done quickly, so I can leave this *equakeiel*." The last word was in the old Dasi language, spoken in falcon lands, of which I knew a little. Syfka's description of our lands was not flattering.

"If you are so displeased to be here," I suggested delicately, "you are welcome to leave and let us conduct this search on our own."

"You would never recognize a hidden falcon without my assistance. Your kind is as blind to Ahnmik's magic as a worm is to the sun." I heard her add under her breath, "You notice it only when it scalds you."

Abruptly she returned to falcon form and took to the sky.

I will return shortly to see to your progress.

The words whispered through my mind like a line of lyrics heard even after a song has ended. I had no doubt they came from Syfka, and the sense of her even so briefly inside my mind left an unpleasant chill.

Beside me, Danica went pale, her body swaying. I moved closer, and she caught my arm, drawing in a slow breath as she closed her eyes.

"Are you all right?"

"I'm fine," she answered. "I was just a little dizzy for a moment." Danica shook her head as if to clear it. "I spent most of this morning practicing with A'isha; perhaps I overtaxed myself."

I glanced from Danica to her guard; Erica looked as worried as I felt. Then again, the sparrow's whole frame had already been taut as a wire. Facing a falcon, against whom all her fighting prowess would not let her win, had left her visibly tense.

Syfka had asked for our help, even though she had dismissed our ability to give any. Harming us now would be sabotaging herself. Wouldn't it?

Still, we couldn't be too careful. "I think we should try to get a better sense of what Syfka is capable of before she returns—and, if possible, learn something about her criminal, or at least get an idea of how and where he or she might be hiding," I said.

Danica nodded, but admitted, "Falcon contempt for outsiders is legendary. Even though we had an agreement with them during the war, we were never in a position to demand much in the way of concrete information. They certainly didn't speak of criminals or illusion spells." Her color had returned somewhat, and her voice was again confident. Only fatigue, I hoped. "Don't the falcons and the serpiente share origins?"

"Technically," I said, reluctant to revisit past grief, "but we have had almost no contact since Maeve's coven split ... thousands of years ago. Most of the records we do have are either embedded in myth, or so old that they are almost impossible to read even if one knows the language."

"Almost no contact?" Danica asked gently.

"My oldest brother, Anjay, was heir before I ..." I took a breath, trying to clear too many memories from my mind. "I don't know how he encountered Syfka, but she brought him to Ahnmik and he was allowed an audience with their Empress, so he could petition for her aid in the war."

Danica knew as well as I did that the falcons had given my kind no help. "What happened?"

"I don't know. . . . He never had a chance to tell us."

The moment Anjay had returned to our lands, he had been told about the death of our sister Sisal—the horrible, senseless slaughter of mother and child that had sent him in a fury to the Keep.

His body had never been recovered.

I did not tell Danica the rest of that story. Anjay had gone to avenge our sister's death by killing Danica's mother, Tuuli Thea at the time. I did not want to know whether he had succeeded in harming any of the avian people before he died. I did not want to know whether one of the Royal Flight—Andreios, perhaps—had ended Anjay's life. It was for the best that Anjay had failed, but I had still lost a brother that day four years ago.

When I had arrived home and learned of this terrible series of events, I had immediately set out for the Hawk's Keep. I had started that ride in a fog of denial, refusing to acknowledge that my brother was dead, refusing to believe that the burden of the royal seat had fallen to me so suddenly at the age of sixteen. The hours had turned my thoughts from disbelief to mad fury. I had scaled the walls of the Hawk's Keep, intent on murder, and stumbled into the room of Danica Shardae.

And there, I think I fell in love. As I beheld the avian princess sleeping so innocently, her cheek marked by a new cut—probably by one of my own people's blades—my hatred died, leaving only a desperate desire for peace in its wake. When the mad suggestion was made last winter that taking the enemy queen as my mate could end the war, it had almost seemed like fate. It had not been easy to bridge the gaps between us, but together we had managed.

Fate had given me many gifts. Danica Shardae was the one for which I would forever be most grateful.

Erica drew me from my musing as she offered tentatively, "The scholar Valene studied in falcon lands once. I lost touch with her after I joined the Royal Flight, but someone might know her whereabouts."

Excellent. "Danica?"

"Yes? Oh . . . sorry," she answered, smiling tiredly. "I seem to be a bit useless today. I haven't heard from Valene in years, but Andreios would probably be able to find her."

"You're dancing tonight, aren't you?" I asked. Though Danica had performed some simple improvisational dances at Namir-da eight months before, I had never been allowed to watch her practice with A'isha, leader of the dancers' guild and the only one daring enough to teach the serpiente art to an avian queen. That night was to be Danica's first performance of the more complex, traditional dances. Even if fatigue was her only ailment, that could stop her from taking the stage.

Danica nodded. "The thought has me so nervous I feel ill, even if the performance is only for A'isha, you and a few of the other dancers who have practiced with me," she confided.

"Why don't you get some rest? I can track down Andreios and ask him about Valene. If I see A'isha, I'll also find out whether her guild knows anything about a hidden falcon."

"Perhaps that's a good idea."

Without being told, Erica stayed beside her queen. I hoped this spell was truly a combination of nerves and fatigue, but I could not help the sense of unease gnawing at my mind.

I asked two people before I believed that Andreios was with A'isha in the synkal—where the reserved leader of the Royal Flight apparently spent most of his free time in serpiente lands. Despite the warning, the scene on the dais was a shock.

A'isha and Rei were facing each other with their hands touching, poised to begin one of the simpler dances. I could barely hear the faint melody A'isha was singing, a wordless tune meant to imitate the flute that would normally play.

The two moved into the dance seamlessly enough to suggest weeks of practice—the last thing I would expect of the crow. I wondered if Danica knew that her teacher had found two students instead of one.

I closed the synkal door loudly behind me, as if I had just entered. Both dancers jumped and turned to face me.

A'isha recovered first. The viper slithered down from the synkal dais, the movement sliding the material of her dress enough that one of her legs was bared to the thigh for a moment.

Rei wasn't watching the show, which was obviously put on for his benefit. He descended the stairs with a haughty expression that dared me to comment.

I knew better than to bait him now. If I even implied that I had been watching, A'isha would probably never get the conservative crow onto her stage again.

Why she had made the effort to teach him in the first place was a mystery to me. A'isha was notoriously picky in her choice of students, and although I respected Andreios, he could not possibly share Danica's passion for dance.

Still, I was thankful that circumstances had put together the two people I sought.

"Rei, A'isha, we've just had a visit from Syfka."

All traces of defiance disappeared instantly from Rei's face. "What does she want?"

"She's looking for a falcon; she didn't say his name, or what he had done, only that he was a criminal. You wouldn't happen to know of any falcons in the avian court, would you?"

Rei cleared his throat, obviously suppressing a laugh. "The falcons are fastidiously purebred. Their kind doesn't mix with ours, no matter how similar we may seem."

A'isha responded in the same way. "I can't imagine any creature with wings masquerading as one without, though I was once told that the falcons act more like serpents in their free time than like avian ladies and gentlemen." She shook her head. "I've known most of my dancers since they were infants. No one could hide among them without being noticed. I can ask if anyone has heard anything in the market, though."

"Thank you."

"You're stealing my student, anyway. I may as well find something else to do." She kissed Rei on the cheek as she turned. "Don't work too hard." She fluttered away, leaving Rei shaking his head.

"You seem to have a new friend." I said the words with all the blandness I could manage.

"A'isha has kindly agreed to teach me her art. That is all."

I debated asking more, but unfortunately, now was not the time to push Rei, no matter how tempting. "I came to find you because Erica suggested you might be able to help us find someone—a scholar named Valene, who she says once knew a great deal about the falcons."

Rei looked surprised. "Valene Silvermead is Erica's aunt. She was a well-respected avian scholar who specialized in knowledge of other cultures. I understand she has spent time in human lands, as well as with the wolves and the falcons. She was exiled by Danica's mother for her dealings with the serpiente and ended up living as a recluse on the edge of our land. I suppose the episode dimmed her faith in the avian court somewhat, since she has expressed no desire to return since."

"Could we get her here?" I asked. "I hope to gather as much information as possible before dealing with Syfka again."

"Valene's nephew was once a member of my flight, so I've stayed in touch with her despite the scandal," Rei admitted.

"I remember her as a strong flier. We could probably make it back here by the evening meal, though that's assuming she's home and not off investigating some new land."

"Danica is performing tonight, so we have been invited to dine in sha'Mehay," I said. "When you two return, could you have Valene meet us there?"

Sha'Mehay was the name for the local dancer's nest, where the members of the dancers' guild lived, slept, dined, studied and of course danced. The name most closely translated to *the ones who dance with illusions* or *the ones who dance with eternity*. Outsiders were rarely allowed inside, and even for a cobra, an invitation was a rare honor.

Rei nodded. "I will come find you the moment we touch ground."

CHAPTER 2

DANICA'S NORMAL GLOW HAD RETURNED by the time evening fell, though her golden eyes still held traces of the nerves she had spoken of earlier. Her warmth helped soothe my tousled emotions as we walked together to the nest, her hand in mine.

On the topic of falcons, Danica shared one memory: that of a child the falcons had sent to the Keep when she had been too young to realize he was there to check up on her kind.

"Sebastian was only twelve when he came to us, as a sort of ambassador," she explained. "I remember teaching him children's games, and wondering why he did not know them. When Syfka arrived to check on him, he announced that he wanted to stay and be my alistair. I can still remember her horrified expression before she ordered him to return home."

Danica smiled slightly, though there was a dark shadow of loss behind the memory.

"I learned to fear the falcons later," Danica added, "when my mother first explained to me how critical their help was, and how we struggled not to offend them ... but I always remember Sebastian fondly. In a way, he was the last real playmate I had. Rei's father was killed right after Sebastian left, and finally the war seemed real to me. All my friends began to train as soldiers, and I began to walk the fields. Two years later, upon my sister's death, I became heir to the throne, and suddenly childhood was over." She shook her head. "No matter how much I've ever feared the falcons, when I think of simpler days, I still remember peregrine wings."

Danica paused, and I pulled her into my arms. She looked up at me with a smile.

"Peregrine wings and Cobriana eyes," she said, drawing herself out of the past and into the peaceful shelter of the present. "The two things that come to mind whenever I think of home and safety. Come, my love—let me dance for you."

At this she led me toward the doors of the dancer's nest, a place that held no room for melancholy or suspicion.

Sha'Mehay had been built into the forest, the walls and ceiling formed by heavy nets strung between trees and then covered with leather, clay and finally ever-growing vines. The nets in the center of the ceiling could be rolled back to let sun or moonlight in and fire smoke out.

Even while standing outside, I could hear the rhythm of drums and the flutist's tunes. Once we were inside, the world was awhirl with sound and color and movement. I had come here only rarely before, but even if I had spent all my life in the nest, I did not think I would ever become immune to its wonder. The slate floor was almost entirely covered by layers of Persian carpets, pillows, blankets and other soft material the dancers had found. The only undecorated surface was in the center, around the bonfire that constantly burned to keep the nest bright and warm.

17

Some of the coven were working, teaching their students not only dances, but history. Among the serpiente, these dancers preserved our myths and most ancient traditions. A few, who had been born and raised in the nest, had also spent their lives studying the language that Maeve's coven had spoken thousands of years ago.

A'isha twirled up to us in a ripple of crimson and silver *melos* scarves belted around her waist to form an improvised bodice and skirt that alternately molded to and slithered away from her skin. Each flowing movement revealed bright symbols painted onto her body.

"Danica, *ak'varlheah*," A'isha greeted her student warmly, kissing Danica's cheek as she drew her farther into the nest. "A gift, for each of you," A'isha said as she produced a pair of woven silks the color of beaten gold. She tied one around Danica's waist, then turned to do the same for me. The color symbolized an eternal tie to another; it was an instantly visible declaration of loyalty to one's mate. "Now, I must steal Danica from you," A'isha apologized, "if you wish to see her dance later."

In the back of the nest was a stairwell I had never descended. Danica stole a kiss for good luck before A'isha led her down those steps to prepare.

Meanwhile, one of the other dancers called me over to the fireside, where food was being passed in a ring around the flames, along with jugs of warm spiced wine.

"You made a good choice for your Naga," she assured me. "Danica is more graceful on a dais than half the serpents I know."

"Provided she isn't blushing too brightly to see," another quipped. "The first time I saw our queen perform, I thought she was a lost cause—far too uptight, like most avians—but I'm glad to be proved wrong."

I knew I was grinning. I had never doubted that Danica could learn the serpent art. Much of her loved my world; a part of her craved dance as surely as anyone else in this nest did. Perhaps that thirst came from her time dancing with the currents of air far above where we earthbound creatures roamed, or perhaps it came from the expressive nature her own world forced her to hide.

Similar conversation flowed among us until A'isha's musical voice commanded me, "Zane, admire your queen."

The words brought our attention to the back of the room, where Danica had emerged, looking so beautiful that she took my breath away.

In response to her teacher's words, Danica smiled and shook her head, causing her golden hair to ripple about her face. It made my heart speed and my breath still, as if I was afraid the next movement would shatter the world.

She was a spark of fire in sha'Mehay. The serpiente dress rippled around the hawk's long legs, the fabric so light it moved with the slightest shift of air. The bodice was burgundy silk; it laced up the front with a black ribbon, and though it was more modest than many dancers' costumes, it still revealed enough cream-and-roses skin to tantalize the imagination. On Danica's right temple, A'isha had painted a symbol for courage; beneath her left collarbone lay the symbols for *san'Anhamirak,* abandon and freedom.

"You dance every day with the wind. This is not so different," A'isha said encouragingly to Danica. "Now, look at the man you love and dance for him."

The nest hushed, faces turning to their Naga. Her cheeks

19

held more color than usual, which A'isha addressed with a common dancers' proverb. "There is no place for shame, Danica. If Anhamirak had not wanted beauty admired, she would not have made our eyes desire it. You are art."

Danica stepped out of A'isha's grip. "If my mother could see me now," she murmured, but she smiled as she said it.

"Feel the beat. It is the wind," A'isha directed. "Fly with it."

The soft beat of a drum, paired with the lilting melody of a flute, filled the room as Danica stepped onto the dais at the back of the nest.

Closing her eyes, Danica stretched upward, moving onto the balls of her feet, wrists crossed high above her head, and paused there for a heartbeat. The pose was known as a prayer—a dancer's call for guidance from the powers that be.

She moved into the dance flawlessly, the sway of her body as fluid as water over stone. This was the magic of the serpent and the snake charmer combined, as pure and intense as a thunderstorm.

The first dance was soft and gentle, a common *sakkri'nira*. I could feel the drive in the music, however, and knew the moment when the first dance would move into a more complex one.

When the flute stilled, Danica rose once again onto the balls of her feet for an instant. She smiled at me before she began the most complex of the *intre'marl*: Maeve's solo from the Namir-da.

What had been praise and beauty became passion. Maeve's dance was a seduction, and the way Danica held my eyes made me feel it. Seeing my mate perform those steps made me want to join her, as any royal-born serpiente would.

The holiday for which the Namir-da had been named was still four months away; she would be able to perform then, and I with her, in a ritual that dated back to the creation of my kind.

The music was softening, in prelude to the end, when Danica stumbled, losing the beat precariously close to the edge of the dais. I crossed the room without a thought and caught her with barely enough time to brace myself and keep us both from tumbling to the floor. My heart was pounding painfully beneath my ribs.

A'isha had followed me, and she seemed instantly relieved when she saw that I had caught her charge. "Danica, are you . . ." She broke off when it became obvious that Danica could not hear her.

There was no blood, no wound. I cradled Danica against my chest. "Danica?"

Avians didn't faint. Their systems utilized oxygen at a rate fast enough to keep the body supplied during a long flight against wind. Danica had only ever passed out from poisoning—assassination attempts, to be exact, during the tumultuous time after we had first declared the war between our civilizations over.

"Ooh." The light sound escaped from her throat, and her eyes fluttered open—golden eyes, a shade darker than her hair. Her brow creased with confusion.

"Zane." Danica's voice was tentative, as if she wasn't quite sure how she had gotten there. She smiled wryly and started to sit up.

The movement was aborted; one hand flew to her forehead, and she fell back, taking one deep breath after another.

"What happened?" I tried to keep the worry from my

voice as I looked frantically around the nest, searching for threats. The other dancers were watching us from a careful distance.

"I'll . . . be okay," Danica asserted. "I was just . . . dizzy." She accepted help standing, but once she was up, her balance seemed to return quickly; she rested one hand on my arm, though I sensed that touch was more from habit than weakness.

A'isha looked from one of us to the other, and her expression slid from worried to startled to amused. "Little hawk, you've never been faint before," the dancer said.

"It's hot in here, and I've been tired and nervous," Danica argued. "Perhaps this was too much." She tucked her head down, suddenly realizing that she had fainted in front of an audience.

"Bring her to rest, Zane," A'isha ordered, apparently not daunted by the fact that she was addressing her king. Inside the nest, no one ever was. "I hear your sister's mate makes an excellent raspberry-ginger tea. I suggest you get the recipe. Now off with you."

A'isha's hinted meaning suddenly dawned on me, and I could not help pulling Danica against me to kiss her. "Is she right?" I asked, my mind tumbling with too many thoughts to put into words.

"I don't know what she's talking about," Danica responded, leaning against me. "I hate raspberry tea."

I tried not to laugh; Danica's innocence asserted itself at odd moments, and right now nothing could keep me from grinning. "Danica, Danica . . ." Concerns returned abruptly when I touched her skin. Serpiente were cold-blooded, but Danica was a hawk; her skin was always warm, almost hot. Now it was dangerously chilled. "You're cold."

"I'm just tired," she protested, but I could feel her shivering.

All delight disappeared.

"A'isha?"

The dancer came quickly to my side. "Yes?"

"Would you send some of the Royal Flight to the Keep for Danica's doctor?" Saying the words made any problem more real somehow, more frightening.

A'isha frowned. "Of course. Meanwhile, your mate may rest downstairs."

Danica pushed away. "Zane, I'm not—"

"Danica, you can fly for hours under the Mediterranean sun without being winded; dancing shouldn't leave you this drawn," I pointed out. "The nest is designed to hold in warmth; it is never cold."

I understood her refusal to acknowledge any problem. The last thing either of us wanted to imagine was that something was wrong.

Please, let it be simple. Please, let it be . . . I cut the thought off. I knew what I wanted Danica's ailment to be, what A'isha thought it was, still I feared the worst.

CHAPTER 3

BEFORE WE REACHED THE STAIRS at the back of the nest, we heard bright voices by the front door, a chorus of welcomes as the dancers one by one recognized the newcomer. Danica turned slowly, forcing me to do the same.

I caught a glimpse of a dark-haired avian woman wearing a vibrant blue dress in a style I had never seen before. She was talking animatedly with A'isha, and though I recognized the old language, I could not follow a word. The newcomer spoke it fluently, as almost no one did these days.

Eventually A'isha shook her head, admitting, "I've been studying the old language since I was a child, but you've surpassed me."

The stranger beamed. "I never could have managed without your teachings."

Danica blinked with surprise. "Valene?"

The raven turned, excusing herself from the dancers to greet Danica and me with a curtsy. Rei walked behind her, obviously a little uncomfortable inside sha'Mehay. For a moment I wondered why he had been allowed inside at all—

guards were let into the nest even more rarely than cobras—
and then I recalled that A'isha was teaching him.

"Milady Shardae. Diente Zane," Valene greeted us. "It is
good to see you both."

A'isha followed her and gave the raven a knowing glance.
"Your Tuuli Thea was about to go lie down; she was feeling
faint. Zane, one of my dancers went to fetch the palace doctor,
and another is off in search of a bird to fly the message to the
Keep—Andreios, relax," she said, stopping the crow before he
demanded an explanation. "There is no problem. Zane is
simply being overprotective in the most charming way."

Rei looked at me, but Danica spoke before I could. "I
think I *will* go take a nap," she said softly, forestalling Rei's
questions. "Zane, Rei, I forbid you from worrying. There is
nothing wrong with me that rest will not heal, and you need
to talk to Valene."

"Sensible woman," A'isha asserted.

I was torn between the desire to accompany Danica and
the knowledge that Syfka would return too soon.

"I'll walk her down and stay by her door," Rei suggested,
seeing my hesitation. "If she wakes or anything happens, I'm
sure you'll be nearby."

I would rather stay and forget about the falcons entirely,
but when it came to Danica's safety, I trusted the crow unconditionally. Andreios had known and loved Danica all her
life. Too much the gentleman to speak of love for another
man's mate, he never raised the topic, but only continued to
defend his Tuuli Thea as I felt sure he would with his last
breath.

Seeing our anxiety, A'isha sighed. "I don't know what all
the fuss is about," she said. "Women have been having children forever. Rei can take care of her. You have work to do

and your mate wouldn't approve of you shirking your duty when she's in no danger at all."

As Rei had predicted, I arranged to have my conversation with Valene in the room next to the one where Danica was resting.

"Andreios says you have had a visit from Syfka?" the raven asked, as I tried to turn my thoughts from my mate to the current situation.

I nodded, taking a deep breath.

"The falcons have lost someone, and seem to think we might have him. Our knowledge of their world is sadly lacking, and I thought it best to learn more before Syfka returns. Erica suggested that you might be able to help."

"Thank you for the compliment," Valene answered. "Among my adventures, I spent several months as a student on the falcon island. What did Syfka have to say about the lost falcon?"

"Only that he—or she—was a criminal, that he might have changed his appearance so we would never even know what gender he was, and that he might have asked for asylum among our people. So far, no one has come up with any ideas."

Valene explained, "The falcons' easiest magics include illusions so strong they can fool every sense. We would never be able to recognize one of their kind, if he wanted to hide. As for gender . . ." She laughed a little. "I've seen such a switch made with illusions, though I've never heard of it being maintained for much time. Still, Syfka is probably certain that if she names one gender, our little minds won't think to consider someone who appears the other."

"If that's the case, how could Syfka expect us to recognize this criminal?"

Valene shook her head. "I doubt she does. Falcons aren't quick to overestimate anyone else," she added. "Most likely she asked for your help primarily as a formality."

"That kind of formality seems out of place, considering her opinion of our kind."

Valene paused as if considering. "It is hard to explain. On the falcon island, appearances and conventions are crucially important. The polite face is unnerving in a city where torture and manipulation are condoned."

"If you spent time on the island recently, do you know anything about the criminal they're looking for?"

Valene let out a half caw, a barking laugh that crows and ravens had a tendency toward. "The word 'recently' is nonsense, since more than a century may go by before the Empress turns her attention to an unpleasant matter, and asking 'which falcon criminal?' is like asking 'which leaf?' while standing in the forest." She shook her head. "Falcon law is strict. So much as disagreeing with the Empress can get one executed, even if she *was* wrong. The criminal they are looking for now may have done nothing more than accidentally curse in the Empress's presence and then flee her punishment: execution by torture. Of course, no one on the island would dare argue with the sentence. Implying that the royal family is anything but flawless, just and merciful is considered treason, and punishable by death."

A chill went down my spine. Since Danica and I divided our time between our two courts, I had grown used to avian politics, which were slightly more formal than my own, but even Danica did not hold herself that far above those she ruled. Our people had the right to question their monarchs' judgment; their voices had kept tragedies from occurring in the past. The falcon civilization Valene described sounded horrific.

"I could give you a course in falcon etiquette, but no matter what you do, Syfka will find some reason to disapprove of you," Valene admitted. "You'll either be rude or obsequious, stupid or arrogant. Falcons are raised with the idea that their kind is superior to any other. When it comes to magic, strength, stamina or recall, they are."

And well aware of it, I thought cynically, remembering Syfka's arrogance. Even without a history of practicing black magic, the falcons gave the world good reason to hate them.

"My advice is to treat Syfka courteously, and try to see to what she wants without completely disrupting the palace. Also, if A'isha's hints are correct, it would be best if the falcon does not see Danica again."

"They might not respect either of us, but the falcons have definitely shown more of a preference for avians in the last few thousand years," I pointed out. "Might Syfka behave more civilly with Danica?"

Valene hesitated for an instant, but then met my gaze and said bluntly, "In Ahnmik, it's a scandal if a gyrfalcon has a child with a peregrine, even if both are of equal rank. A match between, say, a hawk and a falcon, two very similar creatures, is seen as disgusting; any child born of them is considered mongrel, a travesty of nature. If Danica really is carrying your child, and Syfka realizes this, the falcon will be horrified. I don't think she would harm it, but . . ." She trailed off, then finished, "The falcons prize children above almost anything, but Syfka might not see a cobra-hawk as a child."

I appreciated the warning, but at the same time, I knew my gaze was icy when I looked at Valene.

Would my own people see the match the same way? If our child was born with onyx hair and golden eyes, would both serpiente and avians look at her with disgust for the cross, and sorrow for the loss of pure-blooded cobra or hawk features?

What if the child was born a hawk like its mother, never to spread a cobra's hood? Would I look at it and regret the loss of my own bloodline?

A knock at the door made us both turn to find Andreios already stepping into the room.

"Betsy is here," he said. Before I could even move past him, he continued, "She was scandalized enough that I was sitting by Danica's door when she arrived; I can guarantee you that she won't allow you into the room until she is certain about Danica's condition."

Despite her petite stature and habit of smoothing down the ruffled feathers at the back of her neck when agitated, Danica's doctor, Betsy, was probably one of the most formidable women I had ever met. If Rei said she would not let me into the room, I knew I would have better luck arm-wrestling Syfka than fighting my way in.

"Perhaps we should retreat to the main nest?" Rei suggested. Even though he knew no more than I did, the crow seemed perfectly calm. Avians always appeared calm; it was a talent they cultivated and respected. In situations like this, it was also damnably annoying.

Valene took up the movement. "I will keep thinking, but I believe I've shared all the useful knowledge of falcons I have. I'm sorry it wasn't more helpful."

We started upstairs, though I paused by Danica's door,

entertaining the notion of walking in and testing whether Betsy would really throw me out. I dismissed the idea quickly. One person I would always obey was the very respected doctor who was looking after the woman I loved. I trusted Betsy's judgment, even though we occasionally disagreed on propriety.

CHAPTER 4

O NCE AGAIN A'ISHA GREETED US as we returned to the main portion of the nest.

Her presence was helpful, as I could see most of the nest was preparing to interrogate us. Loudly enough for all those loitering nearby to hear, A'isha asked, "Betsy still has not confirmed anything, I understand?"

"That is correct," I answered. Immediately, several of the dancers who had been blatantly eavesdropping sighed and turned away.

Returning to a conversational tone, A'isha said, "My dancers seem to think they have the right to know everything the moment it happens—ceaseless gossips, all of them. Even so, our blessings go to you, your mate and, if hope proves true, your child."

"Thank you; I will pass the words along to Danica as soon as her doctor lets me see her."

A'isha laughed softly. "In the meantime, you and An-dreios are both welcome to stay in the nest—as I am sure you want to."

The words caught me off guard. Despite Danica's condition and Valene's presence, I had not expected such an open invitation. I understood A'isha's allowing Danica to stay, but although no serpent was ignorant of dance, I certainly did not qualify as one of A'isha's guild.

She must have seen my surprise, because she reminded me, "It has been too long since our queen has been a student of the nest. We have been honored to have Danica here."

The simple words touched upon centuries of history. Long before my time, the palace hall had been the home of the most famous dancer's nest; the royal family had been a respected part of it. Seven or eight hundred years ago, the Diente had attempted to demonstrate his power over the dancers—and as a group they had rebelled.

No one knew for certain who had put the knife in that king's heart, though most believed it had been his own son and heir's desperate attempt to prevent a civil war. The new Diente had swiftly negotiated with the dancers, and though they had supported the Cobriana ever since, they had never returned to the palace, founding sha'Mehay instead.

Now A'isha offered a small package wrapped in white silk. I opened it to find an old coin, strung on a leather cord. The faded symbol on it was barely recognizable as *Ahnleh*. Primarily, it was translated to mean *Fate*, though like many words in the old language, it had a million connotations.

A'isha explained, "A gift, for your Naga. These coins were once worn by all of the *Nesera'rsh*, the priests and priestesses of Anhamirak during the time of Maeve's coven. The *Ahnleh* came to be known as the Snakecharm, since Anhamirak's symbol was a serpent. The *Nesera'rsh* are remembered only in nests such as this one now, but once, such a charm was the only coin a dancer needed throughout her life. It is said that even enemies at war would refuse to strike someone who wore an *Ahnleh*. And once . . . the Naga wore one, too.

"The day Danica stood in the synkal and you announced her as your mate, I recognized in her the soul of a dancer. You two brought peace to two lands that had long before forgotten the word. It is past time for other bridges to be patched; sha'Mehay would be proud to see our Naga—and, I hope, the mother of our next Diente—wearing our *Ahnleh* once again."

"Thank you," I answered solemnly. "I know Danica will be honored."

"It will be the nest's gift of congratulations, as soon as that avian doctor admits the obvious," she said with a grin.

A'isha's pure faith was contagious. As I watched her most advanced students perform complex variations of *sakkri* and *melos*—dances far beyond any ability I would ever have— I found it hard to consider that fate could do anything other than turn the right way.

I sat with Andreios, who also watched the dances with a mixture of shocked awe and clinical observation. I could see him being drawn into the dancers' hypnotic spell even while he tried to stay detached enough to examine the specific steps and moves in each variation.

The nest atmosphere and the late hour combined to lower inhibitions and make me choose my kind's blunt honesty rather than the avian discretion I normally practiced with Rei. Still, our words were light as we avoided difficult topics.

"So," I teased the crow, "what prompted your mad decision to engage in our favorite heathen activity?"

Rei laughed a little with me. "I received a challenge from

a very insistent young lady, who told me she could never respect a man who was ashamed to dance."

"Oh?" I prompted. "This lady wouldn't by any chance be
a black-haired viper, would she?"

Voice remote, he replied, "No, actually." More lightly, he
added, "And I think A'isha might be offended if I implied
that she qualified as a lady by avian standards."

"May I know the name of the woman who can convince
the leader of the Royal Flight to take up such a scandalous
pastime?"

"She's not a serpent," he responded.

Before I could attempt to learn more, Betsy emerged
from downstairs with a tired smile on her face.

"Yes? What have you—"

"Calm, boy," she interrupted. She glared at the surrounding dancers, who backed off, giving us as much privacy
as we were likely to get. "Your pair bond is fine; I believe she
is in no danger. Her 'ailment' is what I know you've already
suspected."

I instantly started toward Danica's room, but Betsy
stepped in front of me. "You are *not* going in there."

I towered over the crow, yet she was still a fearsome creature. With a glare like that, Betsy could have been a commander in an army. "You said she was fine," I argued, despite
Rei's earlier warning.

"She is sleeping," Betsy said. "She's still faint."

"Is this normal?" I pressed, hoping that some of my
questions at least could be answered. "The chill, her faint-
ing...?"

"I think so." Seeing my doubtful expression, the doctor
sighed. "Zane, boy..."

I jumped as she lifted a hand and touched my cheek.

From another serpiente, it would not have been a surprise; from the usually formal crow, it was startling.

"Does my skin feel hot to you?" she asked, already knowing the answer.

"Of course."

"Yours isn't cold to me—it's the same temperature as this room, which by the way is too hot. It's making your people antsy." I had no desire to point out to Betsy that the nest was kept this way intentionally. She continued, "I don't know much about your kind, but I know that a snake's eggs will grow too quickly and die if they're too hot. Your palace doctor has confirmed that your young are the same way. That being so, imagine a serpiente child growing in an avian womb; it would never survive." Without waiting for me to acknowledge whether I understood, she concluded, "Apparently you're both human enough to breed together. Your mate's body is adapting itself to take care of your child. She will be weak for a while, but otherwise she appears healthy. You may see her in a couple of days."

"Days?"

"I've been a doctor since before you were born, and that gives me the right to be blunt," Betsy said. "She needs a few days without excitement while her system is getting used to the changes. Having you in her bedroom is *not* going to help her rest."

Again I grudgingly accepted the doctor's orders, though I hoped that Danica would argue once she woke.

"Andreios, you'll make sure he does as he's told?" Betsy appealed to the crow.

Rei answered immediately, "You know I would never let anyone do anything that would endanger my queen."

Betsy frowned. "You've spent too much time with serpents for me to trust that means you'll obey my orders," she said. "I'll wash my hands of it until she has the sense to return to the Keep. Just make sure she is allowed to rest. I will stay in serpiente lands until she is well enough to travel, in case complications arise. Zane, your associates assured me a room in the palace."

I nodded. "Of course." I wasn't overly fond of the doctor right then, but that wasn't really her fault. Avians, and their fixation on decorum and respectability, sent me to the brink of insanity almost daily.

The moment Betsy was gone from the room, one of the dancers caught my arm. "Well?" he demanded.

The words instantly brushed my annoyance aside, leaving a swell of nervous joy that would probably not go away until the child was born. "A'isha was right; Betsy just confirmed it."

"Wonderful!" the dancer exclaimed. "Before you go disappearing to see her . . . we were wondering about your plans. If the Cobriana are really returning to the nest, the child would certainly be welcome here. I know it's irregular for the Arami to be raised in a nest nursery, but in peacetime, surely the heir to—"

Something must have showed on my face, for the dancer broke off. Serpiente children, unless they were in their parents' arms, commonly slept and spent their time in a communal nursery in the palace or—in the case of a dancer's child—in the local nest. As adults they chose lovers and sometimes mates, but even as children they were never alone.

I answered the dancer, "I don't know what Danica plans for the child." Avian children were raised very differently.

I looked to Rei, wondering if his vague answer to Betsy meant he might let me slip away downstairs, but A'isha had once again engaged him, hooking one of the many *melos* scarves she wore around his waist in an attempt to draw him into the dance.

The crow looked at it with shock. A'isha plucked the scarf away with a flourish.

"No need to be shy, little crow," A'isha said. "If the gods didn't want people to admire you, they wouldn't have made you so stunning."

I got to see Rei flush for the first time, blood creeping into his tanned skin. A'isha flipped her scarf around his neck.

"One dance," A'isha implored. "I'm sure Zane would go elsewhere; you would be performing only for the nest."

"I'm sure Zane would," Rei said dryly, glancing at me.

I shrugged.

"What is your lady friend going to think, if she hears you are learning to dance but are ashamed to perform?" A'isha goaded the crow.

"*One* dance," Rei said, relenting. "And only because I know you'll never forgive me if I don't take my opportunity to make a public fool of myself." He turned to me. "You get out of here and thank A'isha for giving me an excuse to leave you alone."

I would indeed.

Danica's eyes fluttered open the instant I stepped through the door, and she smiled softly. "I was starting to wonder if you were planning on obeying Betsy after all."

"Never," I assured her. "Though I've promised I will let you get some sleep. How do you feel?"

I went to her side, and Danica hooked an arm across my shoulders to steady herself as she sat up.

Danica winced. "I *hurt.*" She rolled her shoulders, as if the muscles were sore.

"I'm sure," I responded sympathetically. Offering the

Ahnleh A'isha had given to me, I went on, "This is a congratulatory gift from sha'Mehay." I explained the significance of the ancient coin and repeated A'isha's words regarding why she was giving it to Danica.

She took the coin reverently, closing it in her hand for a moment before tying the cord into place. "Thank you," she said softly, as she snuggled closer. I knew the words were not for me, but for the nest around us.

I began to massage her shoulders, and she closed her eyes and leaned back toward my touch. My fingertips brushed the feathers growing under her hair at the nape of her neck. There was still a moment of hesitation in my mind every time I felt those feathers, a moment when my thoughts protested, remembering so many years of war when this beautiful woman had been my enemy, so hated that when fate crossed our paths there had been no choice but for me to love her.

She met my gaze now without any hint of the fear that had once been there. Cobriana eyes had once been for Danica what her feathers were for me. Avian legend said that a royal cobra's garnet eyes possessed demonic power, and it had taken a long time for Danica to trust me enough to look into mine. Most avians still shuddered and avoided my gaze.

"I feel ... tired, but wonderful. Betsy tells me—" She broke off, words failing her, and then gave up on speech and kissed me.

"I love you," she whispered—then yawned widely. "Take a nap with me?"

The request, as always, made me smile. When we had first met, the idea of resting with another person was as foreign to the lovely but reserved hawk as the idea of flying was to me.

I was happy that Danica had *not* yet taken me into the

air, but she had grown used to a second heartbeat while she rested. That blessing pleased me almost as much as any could.

I wrapped my arms around milady; Danica sighed, tucking her head down against my chest like a chick in the nest. Having her there calmed my fears and let me drift into sleep.

CHAPTER 5

WE BOTH WOKE THE NEXT MORNING to an urgent tapping at the door, followed by A'isha's voice. "Zane, Syfka is back. Rei and Valene have intercepted her at the nest entry, and asked me to fetch you."

As Danica began to push herself up to join me, I explained, "Valene suggests that we keep you and Syfka apart; apparently the falcons have some atrocious notions when it comes to children."

She grimaced, but nodded. "I'll savor any excuse not to speak with her. I will probably still be here when you return."

I kissed her forehead and hurried to make myself presentable before Syfka stormed sha'Mehay. I met Valene and Ailbhe inside the nest door; they informed me that Rei was outside with the falcon.

By the time I reached Syfka, her mood was obviously foul. Her first words, as our group turned to walk toward the palace, were, "You have white vipers in the palace guard?"

Ailbhe stood his ground, not letting himself be flustered.

"I am the leader of Zane's guards," he answered the falcon, gaze challenging but voice carefully neutral.

"A white viper, a crow from the Royal Flight, and now a raven exile. Strange companions for a cobra king. Valene, what are you doing here?"

"My Diente asked me to stand with him as an advisor," the raven answered.

"Your Diente?" Syfka repeated skeptically. "Last time I checked, you still had raven's feathers on your nape."

"Milady, surely your concerns are more pressing than how I word my answers?" Valene sighed, and the falcon nodded.

Syfka turned her ice blue eyes on me, and I was almost disappointed that she was no longer studying my companions. "What have you determined?"

"I've spoken to Danica, as well as members of the Royal Flight and the palace guard. If there are falcons in our midst, none of us have been able to recognize them—which Valene assures me will come as no surprise to you."

Bluntly, Syfka asserted, "There are certainly falcons among your people. Avian and serpiente armies have been favored hiding places for our exiles since the war began; the turnover and chaos is always helpful. It is harder to hide now that you've formed this hopeless alliance, but they are still here. The problem is finding the right one."

My temper flared. Only too much time at the Hawk's Keep kept me from speaking my mind and offering danger-ous insult. Instead, I asked, "If there are so many, then why put forth such an effort to find this one, at this time?"

Syfka shook her head. "The royal house of Ahnmik has reason to want this criminal back. That is all you need to know."

Trying not to lose my patience, and failing, I demanded, "If you will not tell us anything about the missing falcon, when he went missing, or what his crimes are, how can you expect us to recognize him?"

She shook her head. "I forget sometimes how helpless your people are. Whatever power you once had has become as diluted as your blood."

"Perhaps we're better for its loss," I challenged.

"Careful, cobra. You're as insolent as Kiesha herself—and are making all the same mistakes." I could not tell if the words were intended to be a threat, or just another insult. Syfka did not clarify, but instead demanded, "I'd like to speak to the members of both your armies, particularly Danica's elite—the Royal Flight."

"Surely you don't think one of your people could hide so close to Danica without being noticed," I said.

"Considering your activities until recently, the most useful skills falcons would bring to your people are our fighting abilities, which any falcon child learns early and learns well. Pride would keep most from staying a simple soldier for long, and talent would get one promoted quickly. Given the choice between serpent or avian, most would wish to retain the ability to fly. That makes the Royal Flight the first logical choice."

"Members of the Royal Flight are hand-chosen by the Tuuli Thea and the flight leader," I argued. "They come from well-known families, usually highborn ones. Masquerading as a soldier is one thing, but—"

"All that would be necessary," Syfka interrupted, "is to kill a son or daughter of one of those families and take his or her form, then go to the Tuuli Thea and ask for permission to join. A petty task."

Our conversation was interrupted as suddenly one voice in the market became louder than the others.

"Don't you *dare!*" The command was given by a woman I recognized as an artist, whose eyes were wide with shock.

Raised voices in the market weren't unusual among serpiente, but it was my responsibility to make sure such arguments didn't get out of hand.

"It was just a thought." The woman's son shrugged, continuing the discussion more calmly. "I just thought she might be curious. . . ."

"That kind of curiosity is likely to get you killed," the artist said bluntly.

I started to turn away, when someone else chimed in. "Take your mother's advice; that girl is nothing but trouble."

"You don't even know her," the son replied. "She's—"

"A bird," his mother interrupted.

"Doesn't matter."

I smiled at the son's youthful optimism, but only until his mother pointed out, "She'll have a father, a brother and probably a mate. You touch her, and who do you think will have you on a spit first?"

"No mate," the boy replied, though his voice was subdued now.

"If she told you that, she's a liar."

"Why would she lie?"

His mother threw up her arms in frustration, swearing under her breath. "You think I understand a sparrow? Forget her, boy—you can be assured she'll forget you."

Part of me wanted to interrupt them, but I wasn't sure what I would say. For all we had accomplished in the past several months, the two cultures still clashed—often. Stereotypes were hard to break. Many avian mothers and fathers worried about their innocent young daughters being exposed to immoral, womanizing serpents. That my kind generally *was* more demonstrative than theirs considered appropriate made convincing the matrons and protectors that they were wrong difficult.

By our standards, their young ladies were perfectly safe. There was no harm in a youthful fling. By the standards of an alistair protecting the virtue of his betrothed . . .

Syfka was chuckling beside me. "Well, well, well. Are things unraveling a bit in paradise?" she inquired.

I glared at her before I could help myself, and she only laughed again. "Half a year ago, that young man and the avian lady he fancies might have been enemies on the battlefield," I pointed out. "The inherent dangers of youth will never change. Volatile hearts and ill-advised flirtations can hardly be compared to the hatred and slaughter of war."

"Hmm," Syfka replied, sounding unconvinced.

"You were asking about my flight," Rei reminded her, wisely shifting the subject back to Syfka's original intent. "Though I can't imagine what you intend to accomplish, looking for traitors among that group." Rei turned from Syfka to address me. "Zane, you know there is not a member of my flight who is not absolutely loyal. Not one would hesitate to give his life for his Tuuli Thea or her alistair."

"How sweet—and unlikely," Syfka replied. "But where is the Tuuli Thea? Shouldn't she give the orders regarding her people?"

"Danica's people are mine as well, as I am sure you have heard," I said. "She is unavailable at the moment, but certainly trusts Andreios and me to make decisions regarding the Royal Flight."

"Well, then," Syfka said, relenting. "Crow, I assume you are capable of introducing me to the rest of the avian guards, so I can see for myself."

Rei glanced at me for permission before replying, "I can gather those who are available, if you would care to meet with them this afternoon."

She nodded dismissively. "You do that."

At my nod, Rei took his crow form and shot into the sky.

I needed to get away from the falcon myself, before I did something unfortunate, so I used our arrival at the palace as my reason. "Now, if you'll excuse me, I'll leave you in Ailbhe's capable hands. He can introduce you to the palace guard before Andreios returns." Belatedly, something else occurred to me. "Danica and I are expected at the Hawk's Keep tomorrow, so we can speak to the rest of the Royal Flight then." Half of that group always stayed with Danica's mother at the Keep.

Danica and I traveled frequently between the two lands, acting as Diente and Naga to the serpiente and Tuuli Thea and alistair to the avians. The plans had almost slipped my mind in the chaos of Syfka's visit, but it wouldn't do to delay them—not with the falcon hovering about and news of our child to share with Nacola.

Syfka nodded in agreement.

"Ailbhe," I said, "kindly keep our guest company, and answer any questions she might have about the palace guard."

"Yes, sir." The white viper sounded no more pleased to be left with Syfka than I would have been.

I turned my back on the pair, but had taken only a few steps inside when I heard the falcon comment to Ailbhe,

"There was a time when a white viper would be killed on sight if he dared to show his face inside these walls. How long has Maeve's kin groveled before these cobras?"

Ailbhe retorted hotly, "Charis Cobriana trusted my sister and me to guard her kin—" He broke off. His sister had been loyal in her own way, but that loyalty had led to disaster. In an attempt to defend me, she had tried to kill my avian mate and had instead caused the death of my mother. "I endeavor to be worthy of my king's trust."

I paused, wondering whether I should go back to the pair and forestall the argument that sounded ready to erupt. Syfka seemed to thrive a little too much on conflict in my lands.

"Black magic. Wasn't that the accusation that drove your kind from Anhamirak's cult?" Syfka asked. "The accusation that placed Kiesha's cobra kin on the serpiente throne instead of Maeve's white vipers?"

I spun on my heel, preparing to return, but Ailbhe did not hesitate in his answer. "Zane is my Diente. The Cobriana are the royal family I follow, and to whom I will always be loyal."

"Your own sister was executed for murdering the woman you say trusted her," Syfka said bluntly. "Do you truly hold no hatred for that? Can you really not *care*?"

"I've been instructed to answer any questions you have about the palace guard—not my personal life." It sounded as if Ailbhe was grinding his teeth a little.

"Answer me one question," Syfka pressed. "Your fighting prowess is impressive, or you wouldn't have gained this rank. The mark of a white viper is obvious enough in your features that I saw it instantly; the magic may be dormant in you, but it is in your blood. If you learned to use it—as any falcon could teach you—you would be strong. If you had that chance, would you take the power you should have had by birth?"

Ailbhe spoke softly, almost under his breath, the words cool with fury. "Treason, milady falcon, is in those words, and I'll take no part in it."

The falcon whistled low. "I could have made you a king . . . and you refused. It's good to see that Zane has such loyalty behind him." There was a pause, after which Syfka offered, "Surely you must understand my desire to test you a little. A white viper in the palace—"

"Test or not," Ailbhe interrupted, "I'm sure you'll understand when I assign a pair of guards to escort you while you're in serpiente territory."

"I would expect no less."

And I would expect no less than a push for treason by a falcon. I knew Ailbhe would approach me later about the incident. For now, I trusted him to do his best to keep our falcon's destructive tendencies in check.

My mother had been the first to accept white vipers into the palace, but so far Ailbhe and his sister had been the only ones to accept the invitation. Most still lived in chosen exile on the edges of our land, refusing to return to the people who had shunned them for generations—or to acknowledge a cobra as their king. Luckily, their numbers had always been too small for them to make a bid to take the throne back.

Would it amuse Syfka to see them try? I wouldn't be surprised to know she might try to overthrow the Cobriana out of simple spite.

As I walked the halls, instinctively returning to the dancer's nest to check on Danica, another thought occurred to me: Was Syfka's lost falcon a ruse, an excuse to get close? Might the falcon Empress have planned this interlude with Ailbhe?

If she had, casual offers of power were the least of our troubles. If a fight erupted, all the ability of the serpiente and avian armies combined might not win against Ahnmik's followers.

CHAPTER 6

THAT EVENING, we convened in the main hall to discuss our unwanted visitor. According to Andreios, Syfka had finished her interrogation of the Royal Flight and left only moments before. Though Rei stood at strict attention, the remnants of anger shone in his eyes.

Ailbhe paced near the doorway, his white-blond hair long enough to slip into his eyes and disheveled enough to belie his strictly worn uniform. Clearly his interview with the falcon about the palace guard had been no less frustrating than Rei's.

Danica's brow was furrowed as she listened to Ailbhe's description of his argument with Syfka. Valene stood beside her, now wearing the clothing of a dancer, with shimmering violet scarves around her waist and a sigil meaning "peace" painted on the skin of her left temple.

"I don't think that Syfka will go seriously out of her way to cause trouble," Valene observed when Ailbhe was finished, "but I wouldn't put it past her to try to stir things up a little if left alone. From what I saw on Ahnmik, the falcons didn't seem that interested in our politics. Much of their magic revolves around stillness; they don't usually attempt to cause change, especially something as major as the unseating of a family that has ruled as long as the Cobriana." She seemed to consider her own words and after a moment added softly, "Though I don't know how they feel our peace affects them. The serpiente and avian people have been at war so long, the falcons may consider peace more of a disturbance than a change in the monarchy would be."

Rei sighed. "Valene may be right—Syfka certainly makes no effort to disguise her disapproval—but I'd still like to think we could manage Syfka if we keep an eye on her."

"Toward that end, I'm assigning people to watch her in revolving pairs," Ailbhe said. "I wouldn't let someone in the guard who I thought could be swayed by the falcon's words, but caution is always a good idea, just in case."

Rei nodded. "I plan to do the same if Syfka follows you to the Keep."

I knew there was also a member each of the palace guard and the Royal Flight waiting outside the door, one to be my shadow and one to be Danica's.

"Presuming Syfka isn't lying about why she is here, we should be able to get rid of her by finding her falcon. I refuse to believe there is nothing we can do to help that search," I said, opening the floor to the discussion we had gathered for.

I wanted Syfka out of my land. I wanted her away from my people, and my mate.

I looked at Rei first. "She seems to think your flight would be the best hiding place for a falcon. Is there any chance she might be right?"

Rei shifted uneasily. "She has a point there, though, as you know, it isn't one I care for. Falcons are trained in fighting skills from a very young age. If someone with their talent could impersonate a crow or raven, it would make sense for him to join a group where his ability to fight wouldn't be unusual."

"Crow or raven . . . or sparrow?" Danica's voice was tentative as she asked.

"Yes," Rei admitted, though he obviously wished he could say no.

"I hate to even suggest it, but you sound as if you're describing Erica. You said yourself that her fighting skills were amazing, though she claimed to have had no formal training. And—"

"Erica's loyal," Rei interrupted, sharply enough that people around him jumped. "I know her. She's no criminal." He seemed to realize he had spoken too hastily, and he backtracked, adding, "Valene, you would know if your niece was an imposter, wouldn't you?"

"I would know." The raven's voice was uncertain enough to worry me.

But it didn't worry me as much as Rei's words. They had been too sharp, too quickly spoken. Perhaps he was only defensive of accusations toward his guards, but that alone could be a problem. If he refused to consider that there might be falcons in his flight, he could overlook something.

Though doing so brought up a score of memories I did not want to relive, I pointed out as gently as possible, "Loyalty does not necessarily ensure innocence." I forced myself to meet Rei's eyes as I added, "We've all been wrong before."

The crow tore his gaze away from mine and looked at the floor. Rei had personally vouched for a young guard who had twice plotted assassination when Danica and I had initially made our arrangement—first on his own, and next with Ailbhe's sister.

Rei spoke slowly, every word a little tight as he asked, "What if the missing falcon *was* a member of the Royal Flight, or was even Erica? What would you do? Would you really be willing to turn her over to Syfka, for torture and execution, just because she was born with a falcon's wings?" He looked at Danica, who held his pleading gaze sadly. "Every member of my flight is loyal to you; every one of them would give his or her life and soul to protect you. Does falcon blood really have the power to negate a loyal guard's willingness to take a knife for the queen?"

He knew. Maybe it wasn't Erica, but either way, Rei knew.

"I would never endanger those I have sworn my allegiance to. I would never endanger my Tuuli Thea, or her alistair, or her people. You know that." He took a breath and said heavily, "And you both know that if you order me to tell you, I will. But I must ask you to consider whether you want to make me betray someone who would give everything to keep you safe."

In the silence that followed Rei's words, Valene spoke, her voice holding the same intensity as Rei's as she looked at Danica and me. "As long as you don't know who their falcon is, you can say so to Syfka and she will believe you, but once you know, she will know. You can't lie to a falcon."

If I knew for sure that someone in the Royal Flight was a falcon, I would want him gone. Unfair perhaps, but I didn't trust falcons. I didn't want them guarding my queen or my child. I knew I was being unreasonable, but that didn't make me any more comfortable.

The only thing that kept me from demanding that Rei

tell us everything was my knowledge that Rei would sooner turn *himself* over to torture than risk having Danica endangered. He was loyal to his queen. Could I fault him for also being loyal to his flight?

This train of thought was interrupted as something else occurred to me. "Syfka spoke to you about your flight. How did you lie to her?"

"I didn't," Rei answered. "I told her there was no way a simple crow would be able to identify a falcon unless that falcon came forward willingly, and I pointed out that a traitor hiding in our midst was unlikely to be so honest. The words were true, technically. Then I introduced her to those in my flight who were available. If nothing else, the falcon's arrogance gives her faith in my stupidity."

I looked at Danica. The Royal Flight was hers to command, which meant that, ultimately, this was her decision.

She looked at me and shook her head. "For the moment, we'll let it drop. But if Syfka does start to cause trouble, we'll need to do what is necessary to get rid of her."

Rei nodded, his expression more troubled than I had ever seen it.

"We have some problems beyond Syfka," Valene asserted. "I spoke to Ailbhe about them earlier, but you should hear for yourself." She hesitated, shaking her head. "As you know, when I'm in the market here, I'm a dancer. That gives me a chance to listen to a lot of gossip."

"Go on," Danica prompted when the raven paused again.

"News travels fast," Valene said. "Most everyone has heard that their Naga is carrying a child. But not everyone is happy." She sighed and joined Ailbhe's pacing. Her dancer's garments swirled around her when she turned, expressing her agitation. "People called it madness when their Diente proclaimed his love for the Tuuli Thea, but they thought it was romantic. A child between you two is all well and good. But many people don't want that child to rule."

My hand slammed down on the table as if of its own will, but my words froze in my throat.

Danica's voice rose as she abandoned her normal calm. "Why not? It's their Diente's child."

Danica had only scratched the surface of my horror. I *would not* allow mob rule to deny my child its rightful place on the throne.

Valene turned from Danica to me, as if seeking a more reasonable listener, but she flinched as she met my gaze. She continued cautiously. "The cobra form breeds true with any serpent, except the white viper. So the child of a cobra and a python or boa will always be a cobra. But the child of a cobra and a hawk is a less certain equation. The serpiente don't mind having a hawk as Naga so long as their Diente is pure cobra—the Naga's power is always second to her mate's. But they aren't fond of the idea of a feathered Diente. They are even less fond of the idea that any half-avian child could choose an avian mate, leaving the serpiente throne ruled entirely by birds."

"It gets more complicated." Ailbhe took over. "Many people refuse even to consider that you would let a half-avian child take the throne. They're acting as if you've already declared your sister's child your heir."

Valene nodded, adding, "They might tolerate a mixed child as your heir if he or she is raised serpiente, and if they are assured that its mate will also be serpiente, but . . ." She trailed off, not needing to say what the other side of the problem was: Danica's court would feel the same way. They would want a daughter to be given an alistair—an avian alistair. Even if the child was male, avian tradition would demand that he be betrothed to a suitable avian girl within his first few years of life.

I had worried about how our child would be raised and how people would react, but this abject refusal was too horrific for me to have imagined.

The serpiente were ruled in only a nominal fashion. Loyalty bound them to the Cobriana line, thousands of years of leaders who had treated them fairly. My family had never hidden while soldiers walked the field, or we never would have held our people's respect. They trusted their leaders to keep them safe. So the Cobriana stayed in power, and the civilization survived and thrived.

Loss of that loyalty, respect and trust would destroy the Cobriana. Loss of their royal line would destroy the serpiente. If the serpiente refused to acknowledge Danica's child as their monarch, no number of guards would be able to keep that child on the throne.

I had walked this precarious balance before, when I had declared Danica my mate.

If necessary, I would do it again.

"I don't think we can deal with this immediately." I looked at Danica as I spoke, searching her expression for agreement or argument. "Valene, the dancers have already welcomed Danica and our child. If they can circulate the knowledge that I *will* name Danica's child my heir, I can only hope it won't be as much of a shock when the announcement is made." Even as I spoke, I felt the cold knot of fear in my gut. Our child would be born in peace, but would she live in war? "Besides that, we'll have to wait until the protests are raised specifically."

"Not meaning to be troublesome," Ailbhe answered,

"but how absurd is the idea that Salem could be Diente?" The white viper's words were answered by a roomful of glares, but he stood his ground. "What I mean to ask is, what is your ultimate goal? Salem will be raised without hatred for Danica's people. He'll have no hunger for war, and what's more, he'll have a civilization at peace to begin with. If peace is your goal, your sister's child will still make a fine Diente."

"And what of our child?" Danica spoke in her calm and detached court voice, which she used among serpents only when she was too angry or disgusted to maintain rationality any other way. My hand found hers, and she gripped it tightly.

"Your child may well be born as purely avian as you are. If it takes an avian mate, its children will probably show little of the Cobriana blood. Again, if your goal is just peace, the child could be raised avian—raised to be Tuuli Thea. Each court would have its heir, an heir raised without bloodlust and hatred. You would have peace."

For a moment I could not speak. So long as I had breath in my body, I would see my child on the serpiente throne. Diente, Tuuli Thea—our child would be both.

"Are you mad?" The words escaped me as I locked eyes with Ailbhe. "How could you consider—"

"Zane." Danica interrupted me, placing a hand on my chest.

"You can't be thinking—"

"Would you rather set up our child for war from the instant it's born? If the serpiente reject our child for their throne, then you still have Salem as your heir. If my people reject it, there will be no Tuuli Thea after me."

I stepped back from her, horror seeping into my blood. My gaze flickered to the others in the room. Ailbhe's pale blue eyes would not meet mine. Rei's did, but then he looked away. Valene was watching Danica, her expression unreadable. My mate was the only one who would meet my gaze, her golden eyes pained.

"Out," I said, speaking to our audience. They looked at one another, hesitating. Valene first deferred, followed by Rei. Ailbhe lingered a moment longer, and I was not sure whether he did from guilt or compassion.

Then we were alone, and I took Danica's hands.

"Danica, do you know what you are asking of me? Giving up my child to the Keep, to be raised by strangers, to sleep in lonely silence, to be taught to be ashamed of what she feels and what she *is* . . . and to be betrothed before she can even *speak,* before she can possibly understand *love.*" Danica closed her eyes for a moment, taking a breath. "I will never have a mate but you. I love you. And yes, I will have an heir. But you are talking about taking away my *child.*"

"What else can we do?" she returned. "Zane, I was raised in the Keep; it is not as horrible as you think. And you would still see her—" She broke off, because she knew as well as I that the heir to the Tuuli Thea saw her parents only in formal situations. She shook her head. "Please . . . Zane, is there another way? Anything else that will keep our firstborn child from coming into the world only to see her land ripped apart by war?"

Silence.

"It will be months before the child is born," I whispered, pleading not only with Danica, but with whatever powers might be. "We don't have to make this decision, not yet."

Danica nodded, but still she said, "One queen cannot rule two worlds, even if she is of both."

CHAPTER 7

Danica and I went our separate ways that evening, each needing time to think. I dined with the remnants of my family: my sister Irene and her babe, Salem. My brother-in-law, Galen, had been bitten by a petulant five-year-old mamba that afternoon, and although the poison was not nearly as deadly as it would have been to a human, he had asked to be excused from dinner.

Irene had recounted the tale with a forcedly light tone, obviously trying to keep the mood up unless I decided to share what was on my mind.

Salem lay cradled against Irene's left arm in a shawl-like carrier made of bright silk and lined with fur. She negotiated the infant and her food easily, occasionally humming softly to him when he woke, and otherwise engaging in pleasant conversation.

"Would you want Salem to be Diente?" I asked abruptly as Irene turned back from one of her interludes with the laughing child.

She glanced at me for a moment, but kept most of her

attention on Salem, who had just decided to shapeshift. Serpiente children were born able to take their serpent form, though they didn't have much control over it for the first several months and their poison did not develop for four or five years. Luckily my kind had a high tolerance for all natural venom, or childlike tantrums such as the one Galen accidentally stumbled into that morning could be deadly.

Another potential problem for Danica, I realized, before brushing the pessimistic thought aside. That was the least of our problems and could be dealt with easily enough.

After Salem had calmed down, Irene answered, "I don't know. Though these last few months have been wonderful, I've seen what you have gone through as Arami and Diente. You and our brothers."

I swallowed tightly. Irene, Salem and I were the only Cobriana left. Avian soldiers were fierce fighters, and they had made every effort during the years of war to end the royal serpiente line.

"Hopefully, if Salem took the throne, he would not have to rule over war."

Irene nodded, running her hand lovingly over the black scales. Salem shifted back into human form, reaching his tiny hands up to his mother.

"I would worry for him, but I would not argue with you if you named my child your heir. I do not think Galen would object either, though he too certainly knows the difficulties that Salem would face even in peacetime," she answered plainly, either not hearing or not wanting to acknowledge how painful the question was for me to ask. "It's a bit early to worry whether Danica's child will be female or male, though I've heard that hawks have a tendency toward girls."

I had not even considered that issue, though Irene must

have thought it was the reason for my worry. Traditionally, the position of Diente was male—if only because enemy soldiers would strike first at the king, leaving a queen and any child she carried marginally safer. However, it was not unusual for a woman to be named heir if she had no brothers of age to take the throne. If she took the throne as Diente, her mate was named Nag, and the succession considered exactly as it would if she were male.

"I don't care whether my heir is male or female," I answered. "We aren't at war anymore, so I don't see that it matters. My main worry at the moment is whether people will want any child of mine to rule at all."

After that I spoke quickly, sharing with Irene the fears that had been raised earlier—what I had seen and heard in the marketplace, my fury at Ailbhe's proposal and my shock as Danica seemed ready to agree with it.

I finished, "Was I such a fool to think that things would get easier after the last arrow fell?"

Irene was again looking down at Salem—her pureblooded cobra child. "I remember the day Anjay died, and you became Arami," she said. "You wept at his pyre, but when you first spoke as heir to the throne, you did so very clearly. You took Gregory and me aside, and you told us that we would see peace if it took your life's breath and blood and soul to find it. And now here we are."

"And Gregory?" I challenged.

She answered without hesitation. "Gregory's last sight was the golden hair and eyes of your mate, who sang to him and comforted him so he would not die alone. I think he was the first of us to see the peace you promised."

I drew a deep breath and walked away from the table— too much energy, too much agitation.

Irene watched me pace. Softly she said, "You once thought you could only hate avians. Now you love your avian mate more than life. I think this will be harder for you, but if it is the only way to preserve peace, I know you will do it. And perhaps the result will be as happy."

I shook my head.

Irene refused to back down. "Your firstborn child is a precious thing, but you won't be giving her over to death, Zane. Only to a different life than you might have wished for her. I know it would kill me to give up Salem, but I would rather lose him that way than cling to him until hatred tore him away."

I sighed. As usual, my sister was far more practical than I. Unfortunately, her practicality made the words no less painful.

Danica and I would likely have more than one child. Perhaps, even if the first was raised to be Tuuli Thea and given an avian alistair, the second could be raised to be Diente.

Of course, raising the second child as a serpent would require doing to Danica what would be done to me with our first.

Knowing there would be more children would not lessen the pain of losing my first one—and lost it would be. Even if I saw her frequently, even if she ruled in peace and visited the palace as often as Danica did, she would be lost to me. Avian children were not raised to be as close to their parents as serpiente children were. They were not raised with dance and a passion to live, but with a chaste sense of duty and modesty.

Danica had been raised avian, but now she lived in the serpiente world almost as much as I did. If this child was raised avian and forced to take an avian alistair and remain as Tuuli Thea at the Keep, she would never have that chance.

Irene interrupted my thoughts, placing a hand over mine. "Zane, you of all people know that you need to try before you decide you will fail. You have months before the child is born—if there is another way, you will find it."

I tried to keep my sister's words in mind as I prepared for sleep, alone because Danica had not yet returned to our bed. Instead I found myself counting my fears, until I finally reached the painful end of the thread of indecision: Irene was right. We could try to change the world and convince our people to accept our child's rule, but if we failed, then I would have to let her go to the Keep.

Losing her to peace would be better than losing her to war.

That thought filled my dreams during the scant hours when I managed to sleep, and it twisted into nightmares.

I dreamed Danica's death. In my nightmares she was torn apart by wolves. She fell from the balcony of the Keep, unable to spread her wings because she had to carry a serpent child.

I dreamed that the child was born dead, and I woke with a silent scream deep in my throat. I reached for Danica, but found myself lying alone.

I pulled myself out of bed and went to seek my queen. My guard followed at enough of a distance to afford some semblance of privacy, in case I wished it.

The day had recently dawned clear, and the earliest merchants were setting up their stalls in the choice spots of the market. I passed by an avian jeweler, who was in the midst of setting out his wares with the help of his daughter and her alistair. She ducked her head shyly as I passed, but her father said a polite "good morning."

The scent of baked breads rose from the next stall I passed, this one owned by a serpiente merchant named Seth.

He greeted me with a tired smile. "I don't often see you wandering here this early. Restless night for you, too?" he asked.

I nodded. "Too much so. What troubles your sleep?"

The merchant hesitated, gaze going distant. "Many things . . . nightmares."

I waited a moment, giving him the opportunity to continue if he wanted to speak, or change the subject if he thought it better left to silence.

He sighed. "There is a rumor that the falcons' Syfka is here, searching for someone?"

The skin on the back of my neck began to tingle with apprehension. I answered cautiously, "That is true. Is this . . . a concern for you?"

Again he looked away, and this time I realized what he was doing: searching the skies. He explained, "I respect your efforts, and I'm glad I can sell my goods instead of wielding a blade—I was a soldier until you and your mate ended the war, you see—but that doesn't mean I'm not nervous when I see wings in the skies."

"I see." He was lying; of that I had no doubt.

He shot me an apologetic look, turning his eyes from the dawn and back to me. "Sir, I—" He broke off and turned back to his cart. "Syfka isn't—"

The slowly filling market jumped at a falcon's screech; the merchant went white, drawing back under the awning of his stall as if to hide himself from the circling falcon's view.

Syfka banked, dove and returned to human form not far in front of me. She glanced dismissively at the merchant, then said to me, "Diente, I need to speak to you."

Instinctively, I stepped between Syfka and the vender, though suspicion about his origins made me hesitate to turn my back on him. "More plots to overthrow the Cobriana line?" I challenged.

"If I truly wanted to plan treason, I would be more careful than to do so when you are standing close enough to hear," she replied tautly. "I wanted to speak to you about our missing falcon. I'm afraid the one I'm looking for might be a little more hidden than I first thought and my patience is wearing thin. I'd like to arrange some kind of test."

I sighed, irritated that she was still going through the motions of asking for permission when I doubted my answer mattered to her at all. "So long as it doesn't endanger Danica's people or my own, or interfere with the workings of the palace guard or the Royal Flight, I don't care what you do."

She nodded. "Then I hope to be free of this backward land by sundown."

The thought occurred to me suddenly, and I asked, "Where is your escort?"

"Sleeping," she replied offhand. "Deeply. Consider it similar to the heavy slumber you find yourself in after too much wine." She brushed aside the topic, glancing at the merchant, who had been slinking away. "You were foolish enough to speak my name—not just once, but *twice*—knowing I was in these skies. You don't think I'm going to ignore you now, do you?"

Again I stepped between them, as foolish as it might have been. I did not trust any falcon, but if this man really had once been a soldier in the serpiente army, I owed him something for that service. "I thought you said you hadn't found your criminal?"

"The one I was sent for—no, I haven't. This one is . . . a nobody, half gyrfalcon and half peregrine, void of any magic and hence of any value to you—"

"Or any value to you," I interrupted. If she was insistent on taking people out of my market, I wanted at least to know why. "What is his crime?"

"That is none of your business," Syfka snapped. "And you have larger problems than one *kajaes* falcon."

"As do you," I pointed out.

She tossed her head. "At least I seek a flesh-and-blood, pure-blooded peregrine who I know exists. You—and your delusional hawk you call Naga—seek a fanciful dream of harmony as impossible as a western sunrise . . . and as volatile as Anhamirak's temper."

"I've seen my dreams come true," I replied, unchallenged by her words. "I've seen an end to useless hatred and killing—"

"An end to hatred, oh?" she challenged. "Can you tell me the future, *Kiesha'ra?*"

"No man can."

"Actually, any fool who can spin a proper *sakkri* could show you your fate. But even you, with your stunted magic, must be able to predict what is about to happen on the other side of your own market."

I turned just in time to see the young, optimistic serpent from the day before catch the arm of the jeweler's avain daughter. Her alistair looked up just in time to see his pair bond pulled aside by his serpent competition.

The young lady's face went dead white in response to whatever her serpiente companion had whispered to her.

Her soft reply caused him to turn abruptly to look at the girl's protector.

"Jenna?" the unfortunate young serpent asked, voice small and hurt.

The first tears rolled from her eyes, and though she hastily brushed them away, trying to compose herself as an avian lady is taught always to do, her alistair saw.

The alistair left off his conversation with the girl's father, striding through the crowd—which rapidly parted to allow him to approach the serpiente.

Another serpent, who was closer than I, sized up the situation instantly and stepped between the two. He might have avoided trouble, but he made the mistake of grabbing the wrist of the angry alistair.

Abandoning Syfka, I pushed through the crowd just in time for the would-be peacemaker to be shoved at me as the alistair pushed past him; before I could wrestle around the shocked serpent, I heard the impact of flesh against flesh, followed by Jenna's cry as her jilted serpiente sweetheart threw the first punch at his avian opponent.

Someone tried to call me back as I waded between the two, narrowly avoiding the bird's retaliation. I caught the avian's wrist before he managed to strike the serpent, who recoiled as he recognized me. The avian swiftly dropped his gaze before it fell upon Cobriana garnet, and he yanked his wrist out of my grip.

I directed my angry question to the girl, whose opinion probably mattered most to her competing suitors. "Is there a problem here?"

She shuddered and shook her head. Then she cast a longing, apologetic glance at the serpent before taking a tentative step toward her alistair, who took her hand and kissed the back of it. I suspected that the show of perfect devotion and forgiveness was done for the serpent's sake, to keep him from getting any ideas about the future.

The less lucky suitor shrugged, smiled and said lightly what was probably the most hurtful thing he could think of. "Well, I lost that bet."

Syfka smiled and for a moment looked gently pitying. "It isn't meant to be, *Kiesha'ra*. Why don't you give up this useless quest now, before your dreams have to be ripped from your hands?"

"Your kind hides on its island, isolated from the real world, as unchanging as your god," I challenged. "You have no sense of what war is like. You have no idea what it means to see those you love fall. You cannot possibly understand what it is to fight for what you believe, and how sometimes you have to fight with words and dreams after all the weapons have been put away. You serve a cold god, surviving on his power for thousands of years without ever *living*." Too angry about the useless market argument to be fearful of the falcons or their empire's wrath, I pushed on. "You speak of giving up my dreams. Have you ever, since Maeve's coven split, *had* a dream? Have you ever had anything worth dying for?"

"You could not possibly comprehend my dreams," the falcon replied.

"No more than you can ever understand mine."

Syfka nodded and began to turn away. Then she paused, smiling a little, and asked me, "Do you think your brother was dreaming of peace, when a hawk's knife cut into his heart?"

I went cold at the mention of my brother. "You . . ."

"Anjay Cobriana visited our lands once. He asked us for

power to help him slaughter his enemies, the woman you love among them. Did you think we would not keep track of him after he left?"

Hearing this creature speak my brother's name was like listening to blasphemy, even though she spoke thoughts I had many times considered. If Anjay had become king, would he have ended the war in blood instead of peace?

"It surprised none of us when he took his little suicide trip to the Hawk's Keep. He fought his way through half the Royal Flight—ask their captain someday which of them your brother killed. Ask them why a crow as young as Andreios was promoted so soon. Ask them how long the fifteen-year-old heir to the Tuuli Thea grieved for her slain alistair. Ask them which of the avians cheered, when the young child Xavier Shardae stabbed the cobra in the back."

I recoiled from the image she painted, wanting to challenge her and knowing it would do no good. I knew the evils of war. Danica and I had needed to forgive to end the hatred, but neither of us would ever forget.

Some things I had never wanted to know.

"Get out of my market," I snarled.

Syfka looked past me, and we both realized that the falcon merchant had fled during the earlier chaos. Syfka let out a long-suffering sigh.

"Think about my words, son of Kiesha," she bid me. "Give up before your hopes turn to dust."

I flinched from the harsh beating of aplomado wings inches from my face as she reverted to pure falcon form and again took to the skies.

CHAPTER 8

THERE WAS A STORM OF ICE IN MY HEART, and I knew by the way my people stepped back from me as I returned to the nest that I was showing it.

The faces from the marketplace and the sound of Syfka's condescending voice jelled in my mind so that I paused to try to compose myself before heading downstairs, wondering whether I should wait until I calmed down.

A'isha intercepted me before I could make the decision. The dancer frowned a little as she said, "You're too agitated for a man who has just learned he is soon to be a father." I started to respond, but A'isha didn't give me a chance. Instead she said, "Danica is a good Naga; she will be a good mother. The falcon must do what she will do before you can react to it. Troubles will pass. You will see. Now, dance with me before you wake your Naga and leave for the Keep; it is past time to greet the day that has given you this fortune."

No verbal answer was necessary, though my gratitude for her blunt words was immense. She drew me into the nest and onto the dais where Danica had performed. Had that only been a day ago?

I stretched lightly. I had not danced recently, and I had no illusions that I could compete with those who usually performed in sha'Mehay, but A'isha knew how far my talent reached and was careful what dances she chose.

She was also careful to keep in mind which dances a man did not perform without his mate. Instead she drew us into steps of thanks, praise, joy and hope.

When I finally pleaded exhaustion, she smiled triumphantly. "I will always smile on the day I can outdance Kiesha's kin. *Now* go find your mate, with a light heart instead of a frustrated one." She all but shoved me off the dais, sending me stumbling onto the soft nest floor as I tried to find my balance.

As always, the combination of A'isha's directness and the dance had chased away old grief, irrational fears and words such as "impossible."

Stealing from the baskets kept by the fireside a small loaf of bread and a jar of honey—the simple fare I knew Danica preferred for breakfast—I made my way downstairs.

I dropped everything I was carrying and sprinted the rest of the way when I heard a cry from Danica's room. Shouldering through the unlocked door, I quickly took in the room—empty but for my mate, who was obviously in the grip of nightmares.

I pulled her into my arms, waking her gently.

She recoiled, and her eyes flew open. "Are you real?"

I knew what had happened. When Danica was stressed or frightened, she was tormented by dreams that were so vivid, waking only brought more doubt as to reality.

"I'm real," I assured her, and finally she relaxed and let me hold her. "What was the dream?"

"The first one . . ." she answered softly. "I haven't had it in . . . months. Since I became Tuuli Thea. All this with Syfka brought the past to mind."

I knew only too well what she meant. "Tell me?"

"It happened when I was . . . eight, I think. Back when my sister and brother were both still alive. I overheard one of my tutors speaking to my mother, telling her that Rei was missing, that she thought he had gone to . . . to look for his father." She leaned her cheek against my shoulder, dropping her gaze. "I had never seen the aftermath of battle before. Never seen death. I found Rei . . ." She shook her head violently, saying, "It was stupid of me to go. Stupid. There were still serpiente there, though they weren't fighting. They didn't care about a crow-child. But a hawk . . ."

She shuddered. "We were both nearly killed. I remember seeing a viper sink its fangs into Rei's side, but . . . not much more. I was knocked out. Rei carried me back to the Keep. Everyone was amazed that he lived. He was only eleven, but he started training to join our army the next day." Softly she added, "We both changed after that. I couldn't get away from the blood even in my dreams, but I felt as if I had to keep going back to the field . . . to try to help, even if it meant just holding someone's hand so they wouldn't die alone."

She closed her eyes, leaning heavily against me. "At least now it's only dreams. I never want to face that reality again."

Fate willing.

Moments passed in silence before she reluctantly asked, "How are things going with Syfka?"

"Intolerable," I admitted. I did not want to detail my

most recent confrontation with the falcon, and Danica did not press. "Luckily, she seems to have hope that she will find her criminal soon. I look forward to being done with this. Do you feel well enough to travel back to the Keep today?"

"We need to," she answered, but despite her tired tone, she was smiling.

"We can postpone the trip if you're not feeling up to it. You and our child's health are more important than indulging Nacola." *Or Syfka,* I thought. She could speak to the rest of the Royal Flight when Danica was ready.

"Don't worry; I feel fine," Danica assured me. With wide-eyed innocence, she added, "I know how much it would disappoint you not to see my mother."

CHAPTER 9

TOO SOON, it was time for the journey to the Hawk's Keep—a ride I normally enjoyed despite my lack of fondness for the destination. I had become used to avians, in general; it was just Danica's mother who made every visit to the Keep a trial.

I put the thought aside, catching Danica's hand to brush a kiss across the back of it as we walked to the stables.

We traveled this route by horseback, accompanied by four of the Royal Flight and two of the palace guard. Betsy, who had never learned to ride, had already flown ahead and planned to meet us at the Keep. Valene had politely asked to remain in serpiente lands, expressing a preference for the company of dancers to that of the woman and court who had shunned her years before.

The mood for most of the trip was light. Our guards spoke among themselves as they rode, sharing stories as we passed through a wood that had once been fraught with death.

"How goes the dancing, Rei?" I heard Erica ask.

The crow reddened, but he answered, "I don't exactly have a knack for it, but I'm enjoying myself." Was she the lady who had challenged him? Combined with Rei's sharp defense of the sparrow when we had been discussing potential falcons, this light conversation made an excellent case that *something* was going on between the two.

"When do I get to see—" Erica broke off, frowning, and said without changing tone, "A couple more just appeared."

At the same time, Ailbhe pulled up alongside us, his brows tense with concern. When he glanced at me, I saw that his eyes had turned pure blue, save for black slit pupils—snake eyes. Even before he spoke, I knew that his doing so would display fangs. Once, I had always traveled in a similar half form, but I preferred to stay in a purely human form when around Danica.

"There's a group in the woods, shadowing us," Ailbhe said softly. "It started as one, but others have just joined them."

I nodded, then sped my horse up slightly to ride alongside Danica. My voice was light, so anyone following us would think it casual conversation if they caught the tone. "We're being followed."

Her eyes widened fractionally. "Who?"

"Not sure." I cut the conversation short, moving slightly ahead of my mate. As Ailbhe had done, I shifted partially, utilizing the natural weapons and armor I always had available. More importantly, the slight change brought with it a cobra's senses.

There were six figures moving together, trying and failing to be stealthy. At least two were serpents; I knew that only by smell. I could feel the four avians by the heat emanating from their bodies. None of them was moving as if familiar with the forest, which meant they probably had not been professional soldiers.

Rei whistled to his people, and we kicked up our pace to one that followers on foot would be hard-pressed to maintain.

A sharp *caw* from the left attracted the guards' attention. I felt the wind on my face as the members of the Royal Flight grew the wings of their Demi forms, elegant feathers spreading in a defensive posture. Ailbhe and Kyler, his second-in-command, followed suit, each unclipping from the side of his saddle the long, blade-ended stave the palace guard used in close combat. I saw scales spread across their skins, Ailbhe's as white as morning frost, and Kyler's brown and golden.

The serpents came from the left, taking the attention of two of Rei's people, while Ailbhe and Kyler confronted winged attackers.

Rei shouted to Erica, "Get Danica and Zane out of here."

Any other time, I would have stayed to fight, but with Danica's and my child's lives at stake, I wanted to take no chances.

Before I could kick my mount into a canter, I heard the fateful *twang* of a serpiente bowstring, heard the whistle in the air, and the wet sound of wood striking deep into flesh.

Danica's horse went down, an arrow deep in its shoulder. I rolled from my own mount as I saw her fall and landed on the soft ground with panic in my chest. Before I could rise, one of the avians thrust a blade toward me.

Had I been in full cobra form, an observer would have seen the famous flared hood with its infamous markings. Quickly I let my natural snakeskin armor ripple into place across my arms and throat, then faced my attacker with slit garnet eyes and a cobra's fangs.

The shift made my attacker recoil. Instinctively I caught his gaze, drawing my blade in the instant my would-be murderer was off guard. Before he could recover, Ailbhe had engaged him, leaving me free to look at Danica.

Two of the Royal Flight knelt beside her, their wings spread across her body, protecting her against other arrows. Was she hurt? Unconscious?

Dead?

She can't be dead.

Rei started giving commands again before I could get to Danica's side. "Erica, get Zane. I've got Danica."

He shoved through the crowd, pausing only to extract his blade after it met an opponent's throat. I only saw him lift Danica in his arms before Erica spoke to me, but I heard the beating of his wings and felt the wind from them. He had her safe.

"Change shape," the sparrow ordered.

"What?" If she intended to fly out of there with me, she was out of her mind. Even to save my life, I never wanted to have my feet more than jumping distance from the ground.

A sound to my left caused me to spin, just in time to face another avian. I felt the sting of a blade breaking through my snakeskin before I could raise my own blade and make a killing blow.

It was not pain that hit me, but something close, something suffocating and wrenching that froze my breath and darkened my vision, as suddenly I found myself recalling that avian blades were often poisoned.

I heard Erica curse as she grabbed my arm, but then the pressure of her fingers on my skin faded . . . along with sight and sound and everything else.

CHAPTER 10

WHEN I WOKE, I found myself wondering whether my head had exploded—or whether perhaps that would be preferable. I rolled onto my stomach and had to grip the edge of the bed until I could convince the furniture to stay still.

It couldn't have been poison. Only one poison existed that affected a cobra that strongly, and if it was mixed strongly enough to knock one out, it was mixed strongly enough to kill.

Was it something Erica had done?

I started to push myself up and suddenly felt hands on my arms. I heard a voice saying, "Don't try to sit up yet."

Warm hands, avian hands. Doctor's voice. Were we in the Keep? We must be. How had I gotten there?

I sat up anyway. The doctor, an avian I didn't know, pulled back from me a little, but offered me water, which I drank greedily.

My senses were returning slowly. Every muscle ached, but seemed to work. I managed to stand when I tried, though I had to grip the bedpost to keep from falling.

The doctor implored again, "Please, you aren't well."

My memories returned, and I demanded, "Where's Danica?" My voice was hoarse, my throat as dry as ash.

The doctor's hesitation made me start to push past her to the door despite the way the world rocked and swayed around me.

The avian finally started talking. "She is still unconscious."

There was more worry in her voice than I cared for. "What's wrong?"

"Her . . . temperature is rising," the woman said hesitantly. "Betsy is worried the child was—hurt."

No.

I shouldered my way past the doctor and down the hall. We were on the Tuuli Thea's floor, and there was shouting coming from outside Danica's door.

"Let me see her!"

Erica. The sparrow's voice was strained as she argued with four members of the Royal Flight.

"She's not to be disturbed," the guard answered. I didn't know these four well, and Rei wasn't with them.

"What is going on here?" I demanded.

I saw the guards' hands fall to the handles of their weapons, but none were drawn.

Erica spun around to face me. "Please, Zane, you have to let me see her—"

"Explain why and I'll consider it," I answered. "I'm still trying to figure out what you did to *me*. That doesn't make me anxious to let you near Danica."

Her gaze flickered from the guards, to me, to the door they were guarding, and back to me again.

Then I felt a rush of power, and the backlash of it as it struck the four guards, sending them falling unconscious to the floor. "I can knock you out, too," Erica said, "or you can let me go to my queen and *help* her."

Falcon.

I knew it, and I had a moment of indecision. Did I trust her?

Did I have a choice?

"Go. I'll be beside you."

Betsy was asleep in the chair next to Danica's bed. The way she was slumped implied that she had fallen asleep as abruptly as the guards outside—probably at the same time. It reinforced my desire never to be on the opposite side of a fight from Erica.

Danica's skin was even hotter than usual, and chalky. It was bruised and scraped from her tumble. Worse was the blood. I smelled it before I saw it, and I had to lean against the door frame, dizzy with fear.

I knew what this blood meant: Even if Danica lived, the life inside her was not going to.

I heard Erica whisper, "Milady."

"Can you do anything?"

"I think so. Give me space."

I retreated to the sitting room, leaving my mate with the only person who could help her—a falcon.

An hour passed as slowly as an eon before Erica emerged, faint and shaking with exhaustion. She barely made it to a chair before she collapsed.

"She'll be fine," she breathed.

"And the child?" I demanded. I didn't know what even falcon magic could do to heal that kind of damage.

Erica looked up. Her smile trembled at the edges, but she said again, "She'll be fine."

I panicked for a moment, thinking she was consoling me

by assuring me again that Danica would be fine, but then I understood. "My daughter?" I asked hopefully.

She nodded. "Your daughter. Thank the sky, she'll be fine. They'll both be fine."

"What did you do?"

Erica frowned a little. "I don't know how I can explain it. I . . . put the hurt pieces together again." She bit her lip, and a little fear was in her eyes as she said, "Your daughter will be fine, but falcon magic is . . . not always the best for a mother. It won't hurt Danica, but this child will be the only one. I'm so sorry."

When the words hit me, I felt too numb to know how to respond to them. Only one child meant only one heir. It meant that if this one was raised in the Keep, no child of mine would ever be Diente. It meant that there was only one chance. Yet I said to Erica, "Would she have lived without your help?"

Erica shook her head. "Danica might have, but not the child."

"Then don't apologize." Death was by far a worse separation than the distance between the Hawk's Keep and the serpiente palace. "Don't apologize for saving my daughter's life. Thank you."

"How do *you* feel?" Erica asked.

I paused to catalog my injuries. "Like I fell off the Keep. What did you do to me?"

"Do you know the concept of force-changing?" Erica asked. When I shook my head, she explained, "It's not a commonly used tactic even among my kind, because it leaves a mark on the user's magic, but when necessary, it can be used for fighting, healing or hiding." Perhaps seeing the confusion on my face, she went on, "Normally you change instinctively, taking with you any injuries you have, and any poison. There was poison on the blade that cut you. If it had spread through your blood, it would have killed you. I forced you to change before it could do much harm, but instead of letting the poison enter your second form, I brought it into myself. *Am'haj* was designed by falcons to harm serpents; it's harmless to my kind."

I would never grasp the mechanics of falcon magic, but death was something I understood very well and was grateful to avoid for now. "Thank you again." Curious, I asked, "Hiding?"

Again the sparrow—falcon, I corrected myself—looked nervous. "Like I said, when you reach that deeply into someone else's magic, it leaves a mark. The power remembers that which it touched. If it remembers enough . . ." She held up a hand, and for a few moments black snakeskin shimmered across the surface. "That is as much as I can replicate of your second form."

"Is that how you became Erica?"

She nodded. "The Silvermead family took me in when I fled the island. Valene's niece and I were very close for a while, but then Erica was hurt. I tried to save her, like I did you, but she was too injured, I was too slow." She shook her head. "It was too late. I barely needed to brush your power to take the poison back, but I immersed myself in Erica's, trying to heal her. When she died, the magic clung to me, so when I opened my eyes . . . they were Erica's.

"Valene knew what had happened. She let me stay, as Erica, so I could hide from the Empress but still live as a free woman. Later I got restless and joined the Royal Flight."

"And you told Rei who you were?"

"He is my commander," she answered. "I told him, and let him decide whether to accept me. I'm as loyal as any member of the flight, sir. You know that."

I knew it, but what would it change? Valene had said one couldn't lie to a falcon. Rei had played on Syfka's arrogance to evade the truth, but I did not know whether I could do the same.

"When Syfka speaks to me again, I can try to—"

Erica was shaking her head. "When Syfka speaks to you again, tell her who I am. She's strong; I don't know how she didn't recognize me already, except that I have not used my magic in years. She'll see it on me now even if you don't tell her, and if she thinks you're protecting me, it will put you and my Tuuli Thea in danger. And I won't allow that."

"What will happen to you?"

"For fleeing the city, and stealing a sparrow form?" Erica answered. "I don't know."

I had a feeling she *did* know. The fear in her eyes said more than her words. But if she didn't want to tell me, I wouldn't force her.

Maybe I didn't want to know.

Before we could speak again, the door opened.

Danica wasn't just "fine." Her cheeks were rosy again, and she stood as if she wasn't the least bit tired. Even the minor cuts and bruises I had seen were gone. She was wearing a simple cotton shift that looked as if it had been pulled on hastily, and the only signs of that morning's disaster were the small bits of pine needles and leaves still tangled in her hair.

She hurried to my side, asking, "Zane, are you all right?"

Her hand fell to my arm, and as I looked at it, I realized I was still wearing my snakeskin—along with the rest of my half form. No wonder the doctor and the Royal Flight had been hesitant around me.

I let the snakeskin recede, as well as the other less-human attributes of my fighting form, and saw Danica smile a little.

"I'm . . . fine." The wound on my arm was minor, especially considering there had been enough poison on the blade to end my life. "How are you?"

Danica hesitated, confusion on her face. "Strikingly well, considering I recall falling off a horse."

I nodded at Erica. "You can thank your guard."

"Erica?"

"Our resident falcon," I clarified.

Danica leaned back against the wall. "Oh dear."

"I'll turn myself over to Syfka," Erica said. "I won't cause trouble."

Danica's eyes widened. "I'm not letting her take you."

"If I may be blunt, milady, I believe this is up to me," Erica argued. "I've sworn my life for yours. I won't ask you to protect me, not when it would only get you killed."

Danica nodded reluctantly. This was Erica's decision, and not one that either of us would be able to change.

"Who *was* trying to get me killed?" she asked finally.

"We don't know yet," Erica answered. "Your guards took down five of them, and dragged the sixth one here. They are waiting with her downstairs."

"We'll speak to her now," Danica decided before I could. I wanted a moment alone with her to tell her what Erica had said about our daughter, but I understood the need to solve this problem first.

Before we could turn to go, Erica suggested, "The doctors ordered your mother from the sick room, but I am sure she will want to know that you are—recovered."

I heard Erica hesitate before the last word, as she realized that Danica did not yet know the extent of her injuries. She looked at me, and I nodded; I would tell Danica later.

"If you will speak to Nacola and assure her that Danica is safe, we can deal with our would-be assassin."

Erica nodded.

"One last question?" Danica asked the falcon.

"Anything you want to know."

"If you aren't Erica Silvermead . . . what is your name?"

"La'Kel'jaes'oisna'wimheah'ona'saniet," she answered quickly, with tired pride. Then she winced and corrected herself. "Or, I used to be. None of those titles are mine anymore . . . so I guess it's just Kel now."

"Thank you, Kel."

Kel left us, and I turned to my mate, catching her hand and drawing her toward me. Again the knowledge that I had almost lost her washed over me.

I would have liked to put off telling her, but I knew this might be the last chance I would have to be alone with Danica before her mother and the rest of the avian court descended. For long moments I struggled to form the words, and I watched as the worry in her eyes turned to fear.

Her hand pressed to her stomach. "The child. Kel didn't mention—"

"The child is fine," I assured her quickly, cursing myself for letting that thought spring into her mind. "Kel says it will be a girl."

Danica sighed with relief. "Then, what . . . ?"

"You were very hurt," I explained. "As was our daughter. Kel saved both your lives . . . but the magic she used makes it unlikely that you will be able to carry another child." *Unlikely.* I used that word to try to soften the blow, but Kel had been honest with me. I needed to be honest with Danica. "Not just unlikely. Impossible."

Danica closed her eyes and drew a breath, leaning against me. "This daughter was infinitely precious yesterday," she finally said, "and she is just as precious now that she will be an only child. As for her future . . ." She swallowed hard. "I want to talk to the monster who tried to prevent her from having one."

CHAPTER 11

WITH DANICA BESIDE ME, I descended the stairs to the Keep's ground-level courtyard, bracing myself for whatever might await me. I had dealt with traitors before. Rarely were motives clear. Rarely was justice easy.

I stopped in my tracks when I saw the woman crumpled on the ground between two members of the Royal Flight.

She could not have looked further from the part of murderess. She was avian, but despite the breed's famous stoicism, the face she lifted when she heard us approach was streaked with tears.

"Milady Tuuli Thea, thank the sky you're all right," she cried, lips trembling as she spoke. "Oh, thank the fates, thank the wind, you're alive. And, my lord, I saw you fall; it's a miracle. . . ."

This litany of thanks continued for a while longer, as Danica and I looked at each other and then at the guards. The spark of fury in Danica's gaze had turned to wary confusion.

"She fought all the way back here, sir," one of the guards

explained. "Then the instant we entered the Keep, she stopped. We explained the charges to her, and she started this. We've been careful to keep her away from the court; we didn't think you would want rumors to start before you could even speak to her."

"I never meant—" The woman cut off her protest. "I complained about the child—everyone has been—but I never meant to hurt it. I'm loyal to my Tuuli Thea, to her alistair; I swear it. But . . . she suggested it, how easy it would be, and I don't know how it sounded so reasonable—"

"She?" My tone was sharp, and the woman winced. I found it difficult to feel sorry for her, though I was beginning to form a bitter suspicion about the true culprit.

"I don't know her name," the frightened avian replied. "Either way, my hands held the bow, and I know I deserve any punishment you—"

"We'll deal with that later." Suspicion was boiling into hatred, and I had no patience for pleas and rambling. "First tell me about the woman who spoke to you."

"None of us knew her really, sir," she replied. "She was tall and fair, avian, foreign. . . . She suggested how easy the plan could be, and after she left we continued to talk and somehow it made sense—"

I didn't need to know more. I nodded at the guards, instructing them, "Take her someplace . . . safe. I don't think she's entirely at fault here. Then find Kel. She . . . went to speak with Nacola Shardae." At their looks of confusion, I clarified, "Erica. Tell her I need to speak to her."

Danica touched the back of my hand as the guards moved to obey. "Zane?"

"Yes?" I turned to her, again feeling a rush of amazement and gratitude for her miraculous recovery. Thanks to Erica.

And fury for her near-death, thanks to another falcon.

"Why Kel?"

"Does that woman seem like someone who maliciously planned to attack her king and pregnant queen?" I asked. My voice was calm, frosty calm—shocked calm. Too much was becoming clear, and all of it was combining to form a shell of ice on my mind. "I suspect Syfka was her mysterious avian co-conspirator, and Kel is the only person I know in these lands who might be able to confirm that."

"Zane, she admitted it herself; she held the bow," Danica argued. "Syfka wasn't even there."

Was I overestimating the falcon's ability? I didn't know how far her magic could stretch. If Erica could shape flesh and blood to draw a deadly poison from me and save my queen's and child's lives, not to mention knock out trained soldiers without lifting a finger, how much more might a royal falcon be capable of?

Ahnmik had once been worshipped by those seeking power. Could a falcon of Syfka's strength control others to the point of making them think that something they would never have *considered* seemed reasonable?

Did that make any less sense than what I had just seen? Perhaps anyone facing a traitor's death might weep, but terror had not been on that woman's face. She had worn the mask of guilt, grief and gratitude when she saw her Tuuli Thea alive and well. She had made no excuses, only tried to explain something she hardly seemed to understand. If she was lying, the ruse was pointless; as Danica had said, she had admitted her guilt.

I shook my head. "At this point, I'm not willing to say whether Syfka could or couldn't have somehow controlled the six who attacked us . . . but even if she didn't give them the idea, I'm willing to bet she messed with their minds a little. The whole group needed indifference to their own lives and callousness toward our child's life to do what they did, and the woman we just spoke to had none of that."

Syfka, I suspected, was more than capable of planning this crime. She had made clear her thoughts about our efforts toward peace, and I believed what Valene had said: Syfka would spare no concern for an avian-serpiente child.

Shortly the guard I had sent returned with Kel. The falcon still looked pale and exhausted, but she had recovered enough of her poise that she did not seem like death walking. Andreios accompanied her. His earlier absence was explained by a bandage on his shoulder; the skin surrounding it had the dark blush caused by poison. He was lucky it hadn't been stronger.

"You want to know about Syfka's relation to our attackers," Kel predicted before Danica or I had a chance to speak. She shrugged and added, "I assume? After all, I'm the only falcon expert you have on hand, and there was falcon magic all over that group." She frowned a little. "I should have reported that earlier. I'm sorry."

I shook my head, dismissing the apology. "You had other things on your mind. What can you tell us?"

"I don't know the exact Drawing—spell," she clarified. "The royals work their magic differently than the lower ranks. But that alone means it had to be Syfka's—unless someone else in the royal house has decided to visit, which I doubt. The last time any of the other three left was—" She broke off, averting her eyes before she said softly, "Back when Alasdair and Kiesha still lived."

Before the avian-serpiente war, then, before a time remembered by any living creature aside from the royal falcons.

"Rationally," Danica pressed, "could she have influenced six of our people so they would be willing to attack us?"

"It would be nearly impossible to influence someone who never had the thought. You needn't worry about Andreios turning against you, for example, no matter what Syfka tried. But if they had considered the act, it wouldn't be too difficult to remove whatever moral or practical inhibitions were stopping them."

"So she could make them bolder, but only if they might have done it anyway?" I asked.

Kel shook her head. "If I took away your love for your mate, your respect for life, your fear for your own life, and your desire for peace, maybe you would kill Nacola Shardae. Not because you would ever rationally do it, but because you would have no reason not to when she next baited you."

I frowned. "So you're saying these six . . . were essentially innocent?" said Danica.

Kel nodded. "By falcon law they would be guilty—guilty of succumbing to another's magic if nothing else, and beyond that, guilty of disapproving of the actions of their royal house. But by your laws, they're innocent."

"And five of them are dead now," Danica sighed.

Every one of us was thinking the same thing, but Kel was the first with the courage to say, "We need to give Syfka what she is looking for, and send her away from these lands. If I had imagined for a moment that she would go this far to find me, I would have—"

Rei interrupted. "You can't be the one she's looking for."

Kel turned toward him, eyes wide. "Is there someone else you know of . . ." She trailed off, shaking her head. "Selfish, idiot hopes."

"You can't be important enough to—"

"Yes, I am," Kel answered bitterly. She took a deep breath and said to me, "You should know. The Empress Cjarsa and her heir, Araceli, command a group known as the Mercy. Before I fled, I was part of that group—specifically, one of Empress Cjarsa's four personal guards. The only people who outranked us were the four members of the royal house. I, along with my working partner and one of Araceli's guards, discovered something the Empress wanted to be kept secret. Araceli wanted me executed just for knowing, but Cjarsa protected me."

She looked away and took a deep breath before she continued her story.

"The Mercy works in pairs. My working partner was like a very close, dear sister. We had known each other since we were seven. She decided that the rest of the Empress's people should know. . . ." She shook her head. "The Empress called it treason. When one of the Mercy falters, her partner delivers the punishment. I refused to bring her in to the Empress. I fled so I would not have to torture to death the woman I cherished most in the world."

Kel continued, "In the Empress's eyes, I am the worst kind of traitor. She had given me her trust and her protection, and I betrayed her to protect someone who had turned against her."

"You can't be the one she's looking for, believe me," Rei implored. "You said so yourself, the Mercy deals with the Mercy's faults. The Empress would not have sent Syfka for you. Turning yourself in would be useless."

As I watched the argument progress, rising in emotion on each side, I could not help feeling Rei's desperation.

Kel could have run when Syfka first appeared. She could have left Danica to die, and stayed hidden. Torture and death—that was what she once had fled. That was what she was willing to turn herself over to now—and I didn't know of any way to help her. I could not protect her at the expense of the safety of my people, my queen and my child.

Kel explained, "My partner—the one who would have been sent to bring me home—is only a step away from death, bound by her own magic in a madness that Cjarsa's wrath forced her into. Even if she was not, do you think they would send any of the Mercy for me, knowing that I left when I refused to turn in another member?"

Rei took a deep breath, trying to regain his composure, and then said very clearly, "If Syfka tries to take you, I will fight her."

Danica began to raise her voice in protest, but Kel was faster. "She'll kill you!" the falcon nearly shouted. "And then she will take me anyway."

"I am your commander," Rei pointed out. "I'm sworn to defend you."

"Not from my own people," Kel argued. "Not when you can't win. You are sworn to defend first your Tuuli Thea and her alistair—and you *cannot* do that if you are dead."

The argument was interrupted as Gerard, one of the Royal Flight who normally stayed in the Keep as part of Nacola's personal guard, landed among us. "Sir, Syfka is here. She is demanding her falcon."

Kel took a breath and looked at Rei with a cool, sad gaze. "Don't fight for me." Then she knelt, taking Danica's hand. "You are my queen, and I have been honored to serve you. If that makes me a traitor in the Empress's eyes . . . I will accept that charge and trust myself to her mercy."

CHAPTER 12

LEAVING DANICA SAFELY BEHIND, I returned to the courtyard to greet our villainous falcon with Kel, Rei and the rest of the Royal Flight to back me. Rei had agreed not to fight, but he had insisted that if they needed to turn one of their own over to the falcons, they would all be there to witness.

The instant Kel had reached the courtyard, she had closed her eyes and her figure had rippled. Erica had faded away, replaced by a woman a few years older, with dusky blond hair, deep blue-violet eyes and the Demi wings of a peregrine falcon.

Syfka landed and returned to her half form with her usual hauteur, rustling her falcon wings as if she was shaking off some miasma from the Keep. The skin between her brows tensed as she scanned the guards and noticed Kel behind me. She seemed to deliberate for a moment and then said, "With such a welcome, you would think I came to take a royal hawk away, not a traitor."

"She is no traitor to us," Rei answered, voice softly dangerous.

Kel put a hand on his arm, urging him to hold his peace, as she stepped forward. "Lady falcon, I would be careful who you call a traitor. The Empress is a just woman. I doubt she would be pleased to know the lengths to which you went to find me."

Syfka tossed her head. "I doubt she will care," she replied. "And as you are no longer among her favored, you will have neither the chance to tell her about it nor the power to level an accusation."

"Are you sure?" Kel asked. "Lady aplomado, you of all people know how precious children are to the royal house. My crimes may seem trivial, if the white lady learns you deliberately—"

"Enough," Syfka snapped. "The child you accuse me of harming is even more of a mongrel than the one your partner bore, and it will suffer the same fate."

I saw Syfka raise her arms in an ineffective defense as Kel lashed out not with steel but with magic. Syfka stumbled, dropping to one knee as indigo bands appeared across her arms and around her throat.

Kel snarled, "Do you think I will stand here and allow you to malign that child? Did you think I would allow you to threaten my king and queen's daughter?"

Syfka had been caught off guard, but now she peeled Kel's magic from her skin. Kel winced as each band shattered, but she let no sound of pain escape from her lips.

"You dare attack—"

"I am already accused of treason," Kel whispered, her breath scarce after whatever Syfka had done to remove the magic. "The sentence is death, and not an easy one. I am prepared for that. I will answer to my Empress when I return to the island, but until then I will not grovel to you at the expense of my Tuuli Thea and her alistair."

The royal falcon's expression shifted from enraged to amused. "You are too willing to be a martyr, Kel."

"I am, as always, what my Empress made of me."

She said the words as if by rote.

When Syfka answered, her voice was cutting. "Then know this: Cjarsa never cared that you left her city. She has not spoken of you since your foolish rebellion. She has forgotten you already."

Kel recoiled, looking more stricken than she had when she had agreed to turn herself over.

Syfka continued, "Did you think a stolen form was capable of hiding you from my eyes? I recognized you the moment I saw you—I simply did not care. You are not the falcon I was sent to retrieve. The Empress has more important matters to deal with. If you are what Cjarsa made of you, then you are *nothing* anymore.

"Stay here if you like. Stay in this backward land, never again to set eyes upon the white city, never again to hear the magic sing. Stay with your rat snakes and sparrows, always remembering you are not one of them, can *never* truly be one of them. Stay with your Diente and Tuuli Thea until fate catches up to them and the bloodshed begins again. Live among strangers and die alone."

She spat the words like a curse, and Kel reacted to them as such, crumpling to the ground as Syfka finished her speech. "Should you return to the city, I will see that you are turned over to my Empress's Mercy and treated as any outsider would be. And of course you know that any child you bear with these savages would be put to death for its mixed blood."

Kel nodded.

Finally, Syfka looked at me coldly. "I leave this criminal with you, but be assured, someone will come for the one I have sought. The white lady will not give up just because I have lost my patience for this search."

The falcon's wings nearly struck me in the face as she departed. She shrieked as she took to the skies, and I heard Kel gasp. When I looked back at the exiled woman, I saw new marks across her shoulders, as if something had clawed through her shirt to draw blood from her skin.

Kel's head was down, her face buried in her hands, and her shoulders trembled as if she was weeping. The Royal Flight retreated, giving her privacy. Rei looked shocked, as if he did not know whether to leave her alone or kneel beside her.

Before either of us had made the decision, the sound changed, and I realized that Kel was not crying. She was laughing, a brittle, hysterical kind of laugh of one who has had a narrow escape.

"Kel . . ."

Rei knelt beside her, and finally she lifted her head.

"I should be dead—for what I did, for what I said to her." Her voice held shocked wonder. "I should have been dragged back to Ahnmik. Never . . . Why would she leave me here?"

Rei answered, "Because she is a falcon, and cannot imagine anyone being happy, exiled from the city."

Kel nodded slowly and reached up to brush her hair from her face. Suddenly she froze and haltingly explained, "I tried to take my natural form, to face her. But I couldn't." She shook her head, grasping a dusky blond strand of hair in her fist. "Once I had beautiful pale blue streaks like Syfka's ... but not now. I've lost that. My skin's too dark, too. I can't remember how it was. I don't know if my face is right; I can't remember Kel, not exactly. I've been Erica too long. Are my eyes right?"

"They're violet," Andreios answered. "Dark, blue-violet."

"At least I still have that." She lifted her head, suddenly defiant. "And I have my freedom. That is all I ever wanted." Then she turned to look at me, with a bit of a smile. "That and to serve a royal house I respected and trusted."

After the tumultuous scene I had witnessed, I barely had the energy to deal with the supposed traitor whose actions had revealed Kel to us in the first place. Especially if she was innocent, as Kel had claimed.

"Andreios, if Kel can assure us that Syfka's influence is gone from her, you may release the woman your flight is holding. She should be harmless now."

The crow nodded, but he looked preoccupied. He took Kel's arm to help her stand, and she leaned against him for a few moments before she took her own feet.

The immediate trauma was over, but I still felt as if I was falling. Syfka had promised that someone would come. Would we lose even more to that search?

We had already lost too much.

"Sir, is Danica well enough to receive visitors?" Rei asked.

He had hardly finished speaking before Danica hurried down the stairs and joined us. Gerard shadowed her in avian form, shifting a discrete distance behind her.

She brushed tousled hair back from her face, then held out a hand to Kel.

"It's so good to see that you remain with us, Kel," she said. "Dare I hope this means I have seen the last of your people?"

Rei tensed, but Kel answered, "I wasn't the falcon they were looking for. . . ." She shook her head. "Someone else will come. Maybe not soon, but someday."

Rei cleared his throat. "Milady, I . . ." He dropped his gaze. "With your permission, I would like to resign from the Royal Flight."

I was as shocked by the unexpected request as Danica looked. She answered instantly, "Permission not granted. Why, Andreios?"

He shook his head. "I've failed you more than once. You have nearly fallen to assassins, and you and your child were both just almost killed. Further, I lost objectivity regarding Kel, and would have endangered you further. I should have told you about the falcon. I should have—"

Danica interrupted him. "Rei, I know you. I have known you all my life." He looked away, but she took his hands and forced his gaze back to her. "You are the best captain the Royal Flight has ever had. You couldn't have done anything differently regarding Syfka, and though you posed your objections vehemently, I don't believe you would have endangered us even if we had not spoken against them. May I also point out that I am *not* dead?"

"Milady, please," he answered. "I am good at tactics; I served you through war and could defend you there. More often now you face deception and disguised enemies, and that is not the art I know."

"And who knows better than you?" Danica argued. "You aren't making sense."

"If you are willing to accept a falcon into your ranks, Kel

would be a worthy leader. She is the best fighter we have. And, while this might not seem like a glowing endorsement, her former position on Ahnmik has given her more experience dealing with problems by means less direct than battle. If you have any questions about her loyalty—"

"I don't," Danica answered.

"Or, if you would prefer another, Gerard has always served well; he is the oldest of the Royal Flight, and—"

"Rei," Danica interrupted. "I will allow you a *temporary* leave of absence, so that you may consider this decision, but then I expect you to return to your duties. The falcons are powerful adversaries, and I have a feeling your faith in yourself has been somewhat shaken. But I remember the day you decided to join my guard; you told me your dream the instant you woke up, after fighting a serpent's poison for days. You took that poison to save my life. You proved yourself that day, and I will not allow a crisis of faith to destroy you."

He looked away again, and his eyes met mine, pleading. I shook my head; this was Danica's decision.

"Leave granted," Danica answered. "In the meantime, if she will serve, Kel may fill in for you. You," she finished affectionately, "may come back as soon as your senses have returned."

CHAPTER 13

"EXCUSE ME."

The cold voice behind us made me cringe for reasons that had nothing to do with falcons or Rei's abdication. Danica turned with a smile, and I struggled to do the same.

Despite how well the recent months had gone, Nacola Shardae still refused to believe that a serpiente man could possibly be the right mate for her only daughter. Because of that, she hated me as only a mother could.

I couldn't quite summon such a powerful emotion for such an emotionless woman, but all things considered, I did not know whether I would prefer to face the former Tuuli Thea or the falcon Empress herself. Unfortunately, I needed to tolerate Nacola for Danica's sake, despite the way her golden eyes never quite met mine. She was discreet about it, but eventually one comes to notice these things.

"Mother," Danica greeted Nacola warmly.

"You have a bad habit of allowing your guards to inform me of important events," Nacola chastised. Her tone was carefully controlled, but it held a hint of the fear she must have felt.

"I am sorry to have worried you; you have found us in the first calm moment since Syfka's plans . . . delayed us."

I regretted that fact even more than Danica did. Immediately our disagreement surfaced in my mind, as I realized that Nacola would ask questions we had not yet resolved.

Nacola just nodded. "You are queen; you had to see to your people first. The falcon problem has been worked out, I hope?"

"For this moment," Danica said. "Kel, who you knew as Erica"—she nodded at the sparrow-falcon—"was not the falcon they sought."

Kel interjected politely, "The Empress is more than two thousand years old. She does not make decisions quickly, nor does she ever hurry. To her, a day, a month, or even a century may as well be an hour. If she is the one who pressed to have this falcon returned, then you may not see the falcons again for generations."

"If?" I queried.

"To Empress Cjarsa, time is all but meaningless. Her heir, Araceli, is more driven. People speak of the Empress's will, but often it is Araceli who gives the orders. If she is the one who seeks your falcon, you may still wait years, or her Mercy may arrive at the Keep tomorrow. And unlike Syfka, they will not be subtle with their methods, or leave until they have succeeded. The Mercy does what is necessary to fulfill their orders." She stopped abruptly, swallowing hard, perhaps as she pushed back memories of her own time in that lofty group. "I'm sorry. I'm so exhausted, I'm having trouble holding a train of thought. Do you have any further questions, or might I be excused?"

"We can speak more of this after you rest for a few hours," I answered. And we would. Kel's descriptions had soothed none of my worries; they had given me new ones instead. "I have a feeling Nacola wants to speak to her daughter now, anyway. Thank you, Kel."

"*O'hena,*" she answered. "You're welcome, always."

Our conversation with Nacola was likely to be every bit as unsettling as Kel's ominous words about the royal falcons.

"Danica, you seem to have recovered well?" Nacola asked first, as we walked back toward a more private area.

"I understand that Kel saved my life," Danica replied. "I feel healthier than I have in years."

"And you, Zane?" Nacola asked, somewhat reluctantly.

"Again, thanks to Erica—Kel," I replied as we stepped into an empty sitting room.

"For that, I am grateful." The moment we were alone, Nacola prompted, "Gerard tells me that I am going to have a grandchild soon?"

"Yes," I answered, and for all my fears, I could not help smiling. "A granddaughter, according to Kel."

Danica moved slightly toward me, and her hand touched mine.

"I didn't think it was possible," Nacola said frankly, "for a child to be born between our two kinds."

"Apparently we've enough in common for it to work," was my terse reply. Both our kinds had human roots. In the best of worlds, the knowledge that we were not so different would dim Nacola's distaste a little.

In the best of worlds, many things would be different.

"I . . ." She trailed off and hesitated for a moment. "I am pleased to hear it." The words came out a bit rushed, as if her determination would only last so long. "I would not wish to see my line end, even . . . I *am* pleased."

Neither of us commented on what we knew was the reason for Nacola's hesitation. She was pleased to know that her daughter would have a child. She was not pleased to know that her daughter would have a *half-serpiente* child.

As Nacola began her questions, I felt as if I was watching a bird of prey circle in the skies, coming ever closer to the moment when it would dive.

"You'll have the babe here, of course?" Nacola said. "Even if the father is . . . not, it still seems right that avian doctors should attend to an avian mother."

I felt myself tense as Danica answered, "Most likely, yes."

I understood Danica's desire to give birth surrounded by doctors of her own kind. The question was what would happen after that.

Nacola let out her breath softly, clearly relieved. "If you know for certain that the child will be female, have you considered an alistair?"

This time I felt Danica's body tense. She answered carefully, "Zane and I haven't decided how we will raise the child."

"Shardae, surely you understand, if you don't give the girl an alistair, she will be seen as outcast from the court. It isn't proper—"

"And if I do give her an alistair, she will be outcast from the serpiente," Danica interrupted. "I said we haven't decided yet, Mother. Once we make our decisions, I hope you will respect them."

The hawk respected very little that had to do with me, but she wasn't about to say that aloud. Gods forbid she say what she was thinking outright. "Of course I must," she replied. Her voice remained even as she went for the kill. "But have you considered what your people's reaction will be, if their next Tuuli Thea is raised as a serpent? The war is over, thank the sky, but it takes more than a few months for the hatred and fear caused by generations of bloodshed to end. Your child might be able to end it, after she is queen, but this first generation will be in a very precarious position. The serpiente have an heir to the throne, I believe. Would you, Zane, be selfish enough to keep this child for your world if doing so risks her right to the throne of the land that needs her?"

Nacola Shardae, damn her feathers, was a true queen. In that single little speech, she managed to hit every vulnerability and fear Danica and I had regarding this child.

Danica stayed silent, leaving me to answer Nacola.

"We will do what is necessary to assure our child's prosperity." The statement hurt as I recalled my conversation with Irene. "We have some time before the decision must be made. If we can find no way to raise the child so both our kinds will accept her . . . then she will be raised to be Tuuli Thea, and I will name Salem my heir until—"

Until another child is born, I had been about to say, but there would be no other child. Danica wrapped an arm around my waist and gave me a half hug, despite how scandalized her mother would be by the contact.

Nacola nodded, and for the first time, I saw a glimmer of respect in her eyes.

"We will decide what we must, when we must." Danica's soft voice cut through the silence. "I hope you will trust us to do what is best. For the moment," she said, changing the subject deftly as her tone lightened, "my most pressing concern is that this has been a long and difficult morning, and I've yet to have breakfast. Perhaps you might join me?"

One thing was true in both our cultures: When a woman carrying a child said she was hungry, people listened. Danica had no shame in ruthlessly using that fact to disengage us from her mother's interrogation.

CHAPTER 14

A S SOON AS THE COURT REALIZED that Danica was well enough to be social, they dragged her into the midst of their gossip, advice and congratulations. The next several days seemed surreal contrasted with the encounters of the ones before. Danica handled the crowds well, though I noticed her harried expression whenever she caught my eye across the room.

I recognized her people's need to be reassured that she was all right. Rumors traveled as fast through the Keep as they did in sha'Mehay, and as much as I wanted to speak to her privately, I knew I could wait until the evening. For now, Danica needed to be queen to her people.

Kel approached me at dusk to discuss falcons and her temporary position as flight leader.

"Every now and then I sense a falcon in the marketplace," she admitted when asked, "but these falcons are always powerless. When they escape the island, the Empress lets them go. So long as they are careful not to have children here, they are no threat to her. I have never recognized one of my own here who would be worthy of Syfka's attention. Whoever it is must be well hidden, or not in our courts at all. If the falcons send anyone else, you may want to suggest they look among the wolves, or other local groups."

I remembered Syfka making a similar comment regarding children when she had described Kel's sentence. "Valene told me that falcons prize children. Even you said to Syfka that the Empress would be upset that our child was endangered in her schemes. Why would a child born here be such a threat?"

"Children on the island are rare," Kel explained. "Ahnmik's magic is based on stillness, death; it does not give life. For any falcon in the upper ranks to be blessed with a child is a miracle. So children are infinitely precious." She shook her head. "Pure-blooded children, that is. Mixed blood children are more easily conceived, but far more dangerous. The magic gets warped in them, and it drives them mad. They usually die by their own hands, but only after they destroy everything around them." Kel shuddered. "I was part of the Empress's Mercy for nine years. Twice I had to bind such children, to try to keep them from harming anyone. It is a horrible thing to have to do to a child whose only crime was his parents' folly."

Bile rose in my throat. I could almost understand why the falcons hated outsiders and mixed-blood children, if they were forced into actions such as Kel described.

"Might the criminal Syfka was looking for have had a child here?" I asked. "Would she have been sent to locate it?"

Kel shook her head. "The Empress has other hounds to do that cruel work."

Her voice was sharp, again laden with bitter memory. I found myself wondering aloud, "Kel, was there ever anything beautiful on Ahnmik?"

"There is *nothing*," she answered instantly, "more beautiful than the white city when the dawn hits it. No dancer I have seen in the serpiente market can compete with the *jaes'oisna* when they perform beneath the triple arches, and no musician in the Keep can ever reproduce the way the magic sings. Those memories echo in my dreams and my every waking moment."

She lifted a hand, and an image appeared, hovering in the air before her: buildings that glistened like the iridescent inside of an oyster shell, roads sparkling with colors too spectacular to name and what I guessed to be the residents of Ahnmik. Each person wore falcon wings, even the little children who ran and tumbled about the streets. As I watched the illusion, I could faintly hear music that was unlike any voice or instrument I had ever known.

"The triple arches are where the dancers and choruses perform. I used to dance there," Kel confided when she saw me watching the city. It turned and tilted to show each piece she described. "Inside the three white towers are the private rooms of Cjarsa, Araceli and, finally, the Mercy. *Yenna'saniet.* When the city is silent, you hear screams from that last tower."

I used to dance, she had said. Suddenly it was clear to me that this must be the lady who had challenged Andreios to learn.

"There are things about my life before I came here that I wish the void would take from my mind. Things I've seen, heard . . . done, in the Empress's name . . ." She shook her head violently. "There is no place more beautiful, but at the same time, there is no place more horrible. And even if I had the choice, no power in this world could convince me to go back."

In the silence that followed, a new question gnawed at me. It had nothing to do with falcon traitors or Kel's future, but instead dealt with my past.

"Shortly before he died," I began, "my brother found a way to visit the falcon city. Were you still there when . . ."

I trailed off, because Kel's face was suddenly stricken.

She hesitated so long that I thought she would not answer; then she said, "Anjay Cobriana. My partner and I were assigned to be his guides as he waited for an audience with the Empress. He tried to change things, in a land that has not changed in thousands of years. It was brave of him, at least. His death . . . was a tragedy."

"Kel?"

We both turned at the sound of Gerard's voice.

"Can I help you?" I asked, giving Kel an extra moment to remove the traces of sorrow from her expression before she faced this man.

"Primarily I've come to deliver a message to the flight leader. Andreios would like to meet with her regarding the position."

Kel smiled. "Hopefully the fool has remembered that his place is as one of us," she said affectionately. "With your permission, sir?"

"Certainly," I allowed.

"Sir, I also have a . . . personal request," Gerard said hesitantly once we were alone. At my nod, he continued. "Traditionally, a member of the Royal Flight must have permission to court a lady, since he cannot swear to guard and protect with his life both his pair bond and his queen."

I had no answers to notions of protection. I still did not understand what differentiated a proper lady from a lady soldier, unless it was the same as what separated a proper gentleman and a gentleman soldier. It seemed to me that avian women needed little more protecting than the men.

I held my tongue.

"It has been difficult to secure a private audience with my Tuuli Thea, and I did not wish to ask inside a room full of court gossips," Gerard explained.

"Will permission from the Tuuli Thea's alistair suffice?" In the Keep, Danica and I seemed to have equal power. The only difference was that in a disagreement, Danica's word won out. The arrangement was much the same as that between Diente and Naga in the serpiente palace.

Gerard suddenly glowed with joy. "So long as Andreios— I mean, Kel—and milady Shardae do not object, your word is certainly good enough, my lord."

"Then court your lady," I encouraged.

"Thank you, sir."

The raven turned as if to start obeying my words that instant, but as I watched him go, a shriek of *ky-eee* froze us both, halting Gerard's steps and draining the smile from my face.

Heads in the market were upraised, and an open area quickly grew as five peregrine falcons dove into the center, each taking human form as she hit the ground near where Danica had been standing with her gaggle of court ladies. The crowd parted like water as I hurried down the stairs to greet the unwelcome visitors.

Combined with such a formal escort, peregrine wings could mean only one person: Araceli of Ahnmik, heir to the falcon Empress—and one of the three who Kel had assured us had not left the island in thousands of years.

CHAPTER 15

T HE HEIR TO THE FALCONS' EMPRESS was an imposing woman, with silver-blond hair pulled back in a tight, waist-length braid, and eyes as clear and pale as the purest blue opal. Strands of hair in similar shades of blue had been pulled out of the top of the braid to frame her pale face. She wore the wings of her Demi form as gracefully as a cloak; their violet-black tops contrasted with her fair skin, while their reddish undersides gave her a nefarious halo.

She wore boots laced to her thighs over black suede slacks, and an ivory low-backed silk shirt with golden embroidery. More disquieting were gauntlets that looked like the golden snakeskin of a Burmese python, and a simple dagger at her hip, no doubt coated with the deadliest of the falcons' poisons.

Her carriage and expression warned that she needed no physical weapon, as did the four guards who accompanied her, all standing at strict attention.

"What urgent business brings the Lady Araceli and her

Mercy to the Hawk's Keep?" I asked, half shocked and half angry.

She met my gaze instantly—a fear of the Cobriana garnet was not for this woman—as she stepped forward and brushed her guards aside. "Cobra, do you claim this palace as yours now?"

I bristled at the words, but forced myself to remain as calm as circumstances allowed. Danica stepped forward, and though she wore a mask of avian calm, I could see the tension in her shoulders and the anger in her eyes.

"I am Tuuli Thea here," she answered, not quite able to conceal her fury. "Zane Cobriana is my alistair, and I am sure you are aware of that. If you are still seeking your lost falcon, Syfka must have told you—"

"Syfka told me many things," Araceli interrupted, "and none of them convinced me that she tried very hard. I want my falcon returned. The aplomado has failed in finding him, and while she faces the Empress's tender mercy, I'm forced to go after the brat myself."

Looking into her pale eyes, I was as lost as any sparrow whose gaze fell on cobra garnet. I found myself recoiling with a hiss when Araceli had done nothing more threatening than look at me. Danica's hand touched my wrist, calming me.

What would the world be like if Kiesha and the other eight serpents from the Dasi had survived as the royal falcons had? Or Queen Alasdair and her first avian kin? What magic might our people have had if we had not wasted thousands of years and countless lives in war?

"It's a pity you aren't still," Araceli murmured. "You might actually remember some of Anhamirak's magic if you stop slaughtering each other for long enough. Still, I see no reason to hurry you back into war; you'll manage it on your own in time. Now, my falcon?"

"We don't know who you're looking for," I answered, glad that I could be honest on that point. Unless I had spoken aloud without realizing it, the falcon heir had read my thoughts a moment ago. Lying to her seemed like a bad idea.

She sighed and then glanced at her guard. "You sense him here, too?"

He nodded. "Well shielded, but yes. Higher."

Araceli nodded. "Excellent." She took a breath as if to sigh, but instead let out a piercing call any avian, serpent or landlocked creature could recognize—a hunting falcon's war cry. Only shock held me still as everyone else in the room jumped, some gasping. Danica went rigid beside me, but before we could consider protesting, Araceli issued an ultimatum.

"If my falcon is not standing before me within the next two minutes," she declared, "I will take this Keep down stone by stone and timber by timber, slaughtering those inside until I find the right one. I suggest you spread the word."

"Araceli—" said Danica.

"You had better hope he's loyal to you," Araceli said calmly to her, eyes glittering with ice. "Otherwise he might just leave."

"Araceli," I said, "you can't intend—"

"I never make a threat I don't intend to keep, cobra. Though, honestly, I don't think it will be necessary. He will come."

I caught Danica's eye, imploring her silently to get out of harm's way. We could not both leave—not with Araceli standing before us—but one could go, if only under the pretense of searching for the lost falcon. Ever so slightly, Danica shook her head.

Out of the corner of my eye, I saw other, less faithful avians shifting into their second forms and either disappearing into the surrounding land or flying to higher levels to spread the word of Araceli's threat.

Kel was the first one to return, her sparrow's form coming to a hasty halt as she shapeshifted at Araceli's feet. "My graceful Lady aona'la'Araceli—"

"You are not the falcon I seek," the heir interrupted her. "You have received your sentence, and Cjarsa has supported it despite my protests. Now take your leave of me. Even this face is tainted by your stolen form."

Kel recoiled, then collected herself and stood at attention beside me. "My graceful Lady Araceli, heir to she who shines in beauty and power, loyalty forces me to inform you that I have sworn myself to Danica Shardae and her mate, and that if you attempt this fight, I will defend this Keep and those within it with my life."

Araceli barely raised an eyebrow. "And you will die, little girl."

"And will I, heir to the kingdom of moon and mountain?"

The new voice behind me made the hair on the back of my neck tingle as I recognized it, but I did not turn away from Araceli. Kel tensed, and I saw Danica's face turn white. Instinctively I stepped toward my mate as I felt her sway.

Again the man spoke. "I'm here. You knew I would be. I too swore loyalty to the Tuuli Thea; you know I did so years ago. I'm sworn to Alasdair's heir, I'm sworn to the descendent of Kiesha and I'm sworn to their people. I never swore to you. So will you take me home to our Empress's mercy? To her torture?"

Kel hitched a breath in as if with horrified shock, spinning to face the speaker. "Rei, careful—"

Araceli was hardly bothering to hide her rage. "Speak not of your Empress that way, nestling."

"I'm no nestling," Andreios sighed. "I may be young compared to some, but I am no child."

"Impertinent—" Araceli stepped forward, her hand rising as if she would strike the crow, but then she stopped, her voice halting. She swallowed tightly before she said, "You're coming back to Ahnmik. Now."

Rei stepped toward her, his face grave. "Milady, you know I will not endanger my people, and I know you will not hesitate to use that to coerce me. So I can only ask you—beg you, if that is what you wish—to allow me to stay. You sent me here when I was still a child. You made no attempt to bring me home when I refused to answer your summons. I hardly remember my falcon form, hardly remember my magics—"

"You're royal blood, Sebastian. You'll remember, when the need arises, and we cannot allow rogue falcons of your strength to wander outside our control."

"When the need arises?" he echoed. "Milady, if I had any shred of power, do you think I would have let my queen fall to Syfka's tests? Do you think I would have let her bleed while I—"

"Enough." Araceli's voice was cold.

"Please, milady, heir to the land of air and cloud, heir to the kingdom of sun and summit, let me remain," Rei said. "Do what you think necessary, but let me remain. Ahnmik was never my home."

"Sebastian—"

"Milady . . . my mother. I beg you."

My mother. The son of the Empress's heir—indeed he must be strong. I could only imagine what he feared, what he was running from, that made him stay here, where he had to hide that strength. There was fear in his voice now, fear not just of losing this life but of whatever would come next.

What *would* come next? Death? Torture? Or simply life in a civilization no person with reason could possibly abide?

"It is unbecoming of you to whine this way, Sebastian," Araceli said. She spoke without warmth to her son. Did her voice hold regret, loneliness, guilt? I couldn't hear any.

"Araceli—" Rei said.

"Enough!" the heir snapped. "My patience is through. Guards, bring him. If he fights you, bind him. Tuuli Thea, Diente, I hope we need not meet again."

Horror lashed me, along with a sick sense of helplessness, as I watched the guards grasp Rei's arms. No words would possibly convince the heir to the falcon throne to give up her only son.

Rei must have felt the same way as I did. He did not fight, but walked with them until they reached the center opening in the floor, where he fell gasping to his knees.

"What are you doing to him?" The pain on Rei's face ripped the words from me. Kel grabbed my arm to keep me from stepping forward.

Rei's form rippled, contorting without any of the smoothness usually associated with a shapeshifter's change. The falcon that finally emerged, wearing the same peregrine markings as Araceli's Demi wings, shuddered as if in pain.

"Force change," Kel said softly. "It hurts, as you have experienced."

"No!"

Danica's shriek—a sound of pain and loss, and absolute hatred—turned my blood to ice. Kel and I were both too late to pull her back as she ran not to Rei, but to Araceli.

"You pompous *hoverhawk*," Danica spat. "You sent him here, you *left* him here, and now after he has proved himself one of us, you *dare* to demand—"

She did not get further. Before Kel or I could reach the pair, I saw the indigo-black tar of falcon magic strike across Danica's face and arms, knocking her onto her back. A wall of Araceli's magic held me in place, so I could only stand by in horror as she drew a dirk from her back and placed the tip against Danica's throat.

"I could simplify so many things by pushing this blade through you," Araceli whispered. "No one would miss you or the mongrel creature you carry." She paused and with the blade of her weapon lifted the cord on which Danica's *Ahnleh* hung. It shone in the light like a mocking symbol of the hope we had held. "Since when does the Tuuli Thea wear a Snakecharm?"

She looked at me, and I forced myself to meet her cold gaze without flinching.

"Danica is also Naga, and a dancer," I said, because Araceli seemed to be waiting for an answer. "The leader of the local nest presented her with the *Ahnleh*."

"I see."

Araceli glanced at Rei, who was being restrained by her quartet of guards, and then at Kel, who was on her knees, shivering as if held by stronger magic than I was.

Finally Araceli looked back at me and sheathed her

blade. "I am a patient woman, cobra." I did not dare to argue with that statement; I barely dared to breathe. "I can wait, and allow you to regret not having me destroy her for you. *Saniet'la!*" she called to her guards and Andreios. "We leave here now."

CHAPTER 16

A

T ARACELI'S DEPARTURE, the air thinned; breathing again became easy, and I fell to Danica's side.

I was barely aware of the guards around us, who had come to their queen's defense and been held just as helpless as I.

Danica reached up and wiped a single bead of blood from the hollow of her throat, where the tip of Araceli's blade had rested. Her chest rose as she started to push herself up—and then she paused, dropping her head into her hands.

I waited for her to look up again, my mind following a train of thought that must have been the same as hers.

Araceli had called her son "Sebastian": the sweet young falcon who Danica remembered with a bittersweet smile because he was her last memory of childhood.

Danica had always wondered how she had survived a serpent's attack, with Rei poisoned and her unconscious. Had Sebastian tried to save Andreios from the serpent's poison by force-changing him and earned a crow's form in the process? Or had the shift been more deliberate, a young man's desperate attempt to keep from going home? Syfka had ordered him to return to Ahnmik on the day Rei was hurt, so no one would have thought to question his absence when the substitution was made.

His recent erratic behavior had now been explained, though I wished it had not. No wonder he had wanted to leave the Royal Flight. If Danica had released him from his vows as captain of her guard, he could have returned to Ahnmik—to protect her, as he always had.

"Danica?" I touched her arm and felt trembling beneath my fingertips. She did not respond, not yet.

Now Nacola hurried into the room and knelt beside her daughter. "Shardae?"

Danica balled one hand into a fist for a moment, shaking...and then relaxed as with a conscious effort. She took another deep breath, and suddenly I felt her force back the grief that had been rising—force it back and lock it tightly away.

As if I was suddenly struck blind, I lost her; she hid her soul from me even more carefully than she had when we had been enemies conversing for the first time.

She lifted her head finally, smoothing her hair back with her hands. For a moment, her face was vacant of expression. Then I saw the blankness drop, and it was replaced by a casual façade that was even more disturbing.

"Well," she said, without a tremble in her voice.

"Danica—"

She shook her head, cutting me off. "There was nothing we could do."

This calmness frightened me more than any blade I had ever faced. "I know." Again, I implored, "Danica, are you all right?"

"Fine," she answered. "It's ... difficult to imagine, that's all. Rei, being someone else for all these years. And now gone." But still there was no more tone in her voice than if she had been speaking of the weather. "It will be awkward losing him."

Awkward? I couldn't even reply to such emotionless words.

Gerard stepped forward, just behind Nacola.

For an instant his concern for his queen was obvious, but then he hid himself as flawlessly as she had and addressed her. "Andreios was a good leader, and very organized. We can make Kel's position as flight leader permanent, and I know at least a half dozen fighters who are eligible for promotion to fill the missing spot."

Danica nodded while I continued to watch the conversation with ever-growing horror. Surely this controlled calm had helped during times of war, when they had faced so much death every day, but I would never be able to endure it comfortably.

"Danica, we can deal with these things a little later," Nacola said gently.

Danica nodded mechanically, standing without assistance. I looked away from her to Nacola, hoping for some words of help.

"Watch out for her," Nacola commanded me, speaking past Danica as if she was not present. "I have not seen her this way since her alistair died when she was fifteen. The only person able to draw her out last time was Andreios ... Sebastian, and it took him weeks."

Andreios—and that was how I would always think of him, regardless of what name Araceli used—was not here this time. Though there had been jealousy between us on more than one occasion, Rei and I were friends. Losing him could not hurt me as much as it did Danica, but it hurt all the same. I prayed to any gods and goddesses who might hear for the strength to see my mate through this. I prayed for the strength to deal with it myself—for my sake, Danica's sake and our child's sake.

Two slightly ragged-looking guards approached us, one limping. They hesitated, looking first at their queen, at me, at Nacola, and then at Gerard, as if not sure who they should address—if anyone.

"Yes?" Danica asked.

"Milady, I'm sorry to have to tell you this, but . . . Kel is gone." The guard swallowed tightly before continuing. "She took her falcon form and went after Araceli and Andreios. Two of us tried to go after her, but we're no match against a falcon. She made us turn back." How she had *made* them was evident in the stiffness of their movements. "But I saw her overtake Araceli's group. She didn't stand a chance. They've taken her with them."

I was too shocked by this second blow to know how to respond. Beside me, Danica also stood silently.

Nacola stepped forward to take charge. "Gerard, you're the senior member of the Royal Flight. I expect you to make sure this doesn't cripple the Keep's guard."

"Yes, milady."

She gave her orders with a natural air of command that I had not seen her assume since Danica became Tuuli Thea. "You two, you've been injured. Patch yourselves up and get some rest," she said to the limping guards. "Everyone else who knows what's going on, get to the market and the court and spread the word that we have lost two of our people. Hear me, I want them spoken of as *our* people, not Araceli's;

they were loyal and deserve to be remembered so. Zane, get your pair bond to Betsy."

Danica tried to protest, but Nacola held up a hand to silence her.

"I will believe that you are fine when your doctor tells me it is so," Nacola stated. "Now go—if not for your sake, then for my granddaughter's."

Betsy commanded Nacola, the Royal Flight and me not to leave Danica alone, and to make sure she ate and slept, two things that she skimped on whenever she was upset. I knew about the sleeping; I had a feeling I would be faced with several more of her bouts of lucid dreaming over the next few days.

Danica's grief at losing Rei was enough to break even the coldest heart, and mine could never have been icy enough.

She spent the first few hours leaning on the balcony, with only her mother for company. I suspected they were sharing stories of the loyal falcon-turned-crow, private stories I had never heard and likely never would.

Hoping my mate was in good hands, I found Gerard in the study reserved for the leader of the Royal Flight, poring through the notes Andreios had left for Kel.

"Andreios was a good leader," he said as soon as I entered. "His files are well organized. He kept up-to-date lists of potential new members—when they first requested consideration, their history, their schooling and his observations. We can never replace those we lost, but I can start interviewing and testing potentials to fill the positions this afternoon." He paused, finally looking up from his lists. "Danica is with her mother, I assume?"

"Yes," I answered. "My presence seemed . . ."

"Intrusive," Gerard filled in when I floundered for words.

Intrusive, yes. I had not grown up with Andreios or ever known the falcon Sebastian before he stepped into the crow's life.

And I could not stand there and share recollections as if he and Kel were dead. I *couldn't*.

"I am glad the Royal Flight is in good hands," I said. "Do you think there is any way for us to get our people back—if not Andreios, at least Kel? Whatever crimes she committed were slight enough they left her here once. Is there any chance . . ."

I trailed off, because I saw the doubt on Gerard's face.

"I have never been to Ahnmik," he answered. "I have, however, had the honor of drilling against both Andreios and Kel, and that was enough for me to know that I would never want to fight a falcon seriously—without even taking into account falcon magic. Araceli held you, me, Kel and the rest of the Royal Flight from going to our queen's side, without even looking strained. Confronting them on their territory would be suicide. If they send our people back, it will be because they choose to."

I began to pace, because this feeling of helplessness was driving me mad. "There has to be *something*. . . ."

"There isn't always a way," Gerard pointed out.

"Not always," I admitted, "but blind determination hasn't failed me so far." As the thought occurred to me, I added, "There is another falcon in the serpiente market, who was luckier than Rei and Kel. Maybe he will know something. I can also speak to Valene Silvermead, since she is still staying in the dancer's nest. One of them must know something that can help us."

"I wish I shared your faith."

"Only Danica needs to. I will see if she is well enough to travel tomorrow morning."

The conversation lapsed into silence for a few moments, and I struggled to find a lighter topic.

Finally, I inquired, "How is your lady love faring in all this?"

His expression shifted, betraying the smile of one happily besotted despite the circumstances. "I think she is as stunned as everyone else, but she is a very strong, capable woman."

I couldn't resist the urge to tease a little. "Strong and capable? Flattering descriptions, but hardly warm enough to merit the soft look in your eyes."

"She isn't a serpent, who wears her passions like jewelry and dances barefoot in the morning," Gerard answered. "She is an avian lady, serene and composed even when she is upset. Strong, and capable." More softly, he added, "She guards her heart and soul tightly unless she is around those she most trusts . . . so every little glimpse she allows me is like the silver moon rising over the sea."

"*A'le-Ahnleh,*" I responded with newfound respect. "My best wishes to you both."

I spent the rest of the day alternately checking in on Danica—who spent the hours either with her mother, or in solitude—and drilling with the Royal Flight. Gerard had sent out missives to a few of the most promising recruits Rei had named, so I was called in to help test their skills.

The loss of its leader was a harsh blow, but the Royal Flight was not easily defeated. Discerning eyes, however, could see the forced bravado and enthusiasm the more seasoned guards showed their newest members.

As evening fell, Danica drifted to my side. Finally true darkness overtook the Keep, and we were alone for the first time since the falcons had been taken away.

I stood on the balcony outside our room, watching Danica stare out over the forest, and not so much as sigh. *Avian reserve*, her people called it, but it spoke of denial, and the circles under her eyes belied her calm.

Although she let me draw her into my arms, she otherwise barely acknowledged my presence.

"Danica, are you . . ." I trailed off, because there was no reason to ask such a question. She was not all right, and if I asked, she would simply continue to deny that she wasn't.

"My mother told me today that one of the Royal Flight has begun to court her," Danica said, and for a moment the statement seemed so inane and out of place that I hardly realized the importance.

Then I made the connection. "Gerard?"

Danica nodded. "I told her there was no reason for him to leave the Royal Flight. He is sworn to protect the royal house anyway, and has always been one of her guards. Swearing his vows as her alistair does not seem like a conflict."

I could see many reasons for it to be perceived as a conflict, but Danica continued before I could voice them.

"She says she is too old to hope for more children," Danica added, "but I doubt that is true. Maybe it would be better for her to have more. Life is safer now that we are not at war, but having only one potential heir to the throne is . . . hazardous. And we will not have another."

The words, and the offhanded way in which they were spoken, made me cold. Logically, yes, I understood the desire for multiple children in the royal house. However, any child of Nacola Shardae would be a pure-blooded hawk and, as such, as capable of usurping the throne as safeguarding it.

Danica must have thought of this, but just as she remained silent about her feelings on losing Rei and Kel, she refused to speak of it.

I broached the first painful topic, because I had no idea yet what to do about the second.

"If you feel up to traveling, I think we should go back to serpiente lands tomorrow. I haven't given up hope that we may be able to somehow bring our people home, and I'd like to ask Valene, at least, if she has any suggestions."

Danica nodded mechanically. "My mother and Gerard have things well under control here, if we travel to the palace."

Her eyes followed a natural bird as it skimmed over the treetops in the warm night air. It dove, disappearing into the forest, and Danica said, "Araceli took them so easily. You really believe that we could somehow take them back?"

"I am not ready to give them up as lost," I answered. I pulled her closer, and finally she leaned against me.

"Idiocy," she sighed, as pain leaked into her voice for the first time. "First I *miss* Andreios, and then I feel foolish for missing someone who was never who I thought he was . . . and then I feel ghastly for being angry with him, when I think of all the times he protected me over the years, and what he is probably going through now."

I stroked her back and she continued. "Then I think of Gerard, and my mother, and I think I should be happy for them. I know I should be glad if my mother has a chance at more children after having lost so many . . . but I hate the thought that our child might then be denied the title she should have without question."

Though relieved that Danica shared my concerns, I wished this blow had not come so soon after the last. Neither of us was ready to face it.

She turned to me and rested her cheek against my shoulder. "You're supposed to be the one going to pieces, not me," she teased.

"You have every right to be upset, and every right to show it, with me if no one else," I assured her.

"It's so hard," she whispered, "adjusting to the fact that the real Rei has been dead for more than half my life. He died protecting me, and I never even knew to mourn him. I was so young, but even so, I feel as if I should have *known*. I always thought his father's death and our brush with our own had changed him . . . but it didn't just change him. He wasn't even the same person. I grew up with Rei, and I couldn't even tell that someone else had taken his place."

Suddenly she shook her head and pulled away from me. "If you want to travel to the palace tomorrow, we should probably sleep." Once again her voice was calm, and once again I hated hearing it.

"Come to bed, then."

She hesitated at the balcony, but then turned and followed me inside, keeping a careful distance.

Even more than I wanted to bring Rei and Kel home, I wanted to see Danica smile again—or even cry. *Anything* would be better than this emotionless poise. Perhaps sha'Mehay and its dancers could revive her, unlike her mother and the solemn Hawk's Keep.

CHAPTER 17

MY FIRST STOP once we got to serpiente lands was sha'Mehay. The dancers greeted us warmly, though we were hardly two steps inside the doorway when I saw the first nervous, questioning glances. We were the first to return from the Keep since Araceli had come. I did not relish the news we brought with us.

"I need to speak to A'isha and Valene."

Instantly, the two were before me. A'isha started to usher us to one of the more private rooms, but I shook my head. The more minds on this question, the better.

"The falcons found their people," I said. Valene winced, and I saw A'isha pale.

"Who?" the dancer asked softly.

"Syfka organized a 'test' to out the falcon. Erica Silvermead revealed herself, while saving my mate's and my daughter's lives."

"Oh, gods," Valene whispered, dropping her head into her hands. "Is Kel . . . they took Kel back?"

"She wasn't the one they were looking for. Syfka would

have left her here, but she went after them, when Araceli took Andreios."

A'isha let out a cry, her face going white. One of the other dancers steadied her, and I could see in his gaze the same pain.

"What was he accused of?" Valene finally asked.

"It doesn't matter," A'isha replied, speaking loudly to the whole gathered group. "He was one of ours, a dancer in this nest. I won't see him slandered, even by the falcon Empress." Instantly she turned to me, demanding, "How do we get him back?"

"He is Araceli's son, Sebastian," I explained. "Her only heir. If there is a way—"

"There *is* a way," she interrupted before I could express my doubt. "Falcon or not, her heir or not, he's one of ours, *ra'o'sha'Mehay*. The Cobriana learned years ago that you don't hold a dancer against the ruling of the nest. The shm'Ahnmik might as well learn the same."

Her determination was infectious. I saw the heat returning finally to Danica's eyes—hope. False hope or true, it was *something*. At least we would do all we could.

"There is a falcon in the market," I said. "The baker Seth. As he's the only local falcon I know of, he seems a good person to ask for information."

"He hasn't been in the market since Syfka was here," one of the dancers told me. "I can check his house, though."

"Please."

The dancer disappeared out the door, but all those remaining kept their attention raptly on me.

"Valene, you're our resident expert," I continued. "Any suggestions?"

Looking the most doubtful, Valene replied, "When I

visited, I heard nothing of Araceli's having a son. Children on Ahnmik are so precious, there must have been a reason for her to let him go the first time. Considering how reluctantly changes are made by the royal house, and how much effort was put into bringing him home *quickly*, there must also have been a reason they wanted him now. I don't know how any of us could discover those reasons, though."

"Any thoughts on Kel?" I asked, though I knew it must be a painful subject for her. "I assume you know more about her history than I do."

Valene shook her head. "I doubt that. She told me once that knowing the reason for her exile was dangerous."

"What do we hope to accomplish here?" The voice rang out from a python in the back of the room. "We've all heard stories about Ahnmik. We all know the myths. We all know—or more rightly *don't* know—how powerful the falcons are. It's sickening that they can just say someone is a criminal and take that person away, but it's not as if they picked up a serpent. They took *falcons*. Two people who, as *loyal* and *wonderful* as everyone keeps saying they were—and I'm not forgetting that Erica, or Kel, or whoever she was, hated serpents vehemently when I first met her—lied to everyone around them about who they were. People call them brave, but does a brave man hide who he is behind a disguise? Everyone gets venerated once they are gone. But all I know about these two is that they were cowards and liars who, a year ago, would have killed me without hesitation. Why should we risk angering the falcon Empress for people who were never ours?"

"I'm sorry, I thought we had accomplished something these last months." Danica's voice was level as a blade. "I thought maybe we were past feathers and scales. We are not talking about two *falcons*, we're talking about two *people*.

132

"We are talking about Kel—a young woman who abandoned everything she knew to save someone she loved from torture and execution. A young woman who entered our world—hidden, yes, because she had to be—in a desperate attempt to have the kind of life we all take for granted. A young woman who used to dance in her homeland, and who teasingly challenged the man she fancied to learn. A young woman who again lost everything, this time because she saved the life of her queen—and couldn't stand to see Andreios taken away without fighting for him. And we are talking about Andreios." Danica choked up for a moment, but before the serpent she was challenging could speak, she took a deep breath and cut him off. "The falcon who became Andreios was twelve when he first saved my life. You call him a liar, and you call him a coward, but you are oceans away from the truth—"

"I'm sorry," the serpent whispered, his quiet words silencing her more quickly than any angry protest could have. "Maybe I'm wrong; I didn't know them. But I still don't think we can save them."

"If they were serpents," Danica asked, "would you be so willing to give up?"

Silence, broken by the return of the dancer who had gone to look for the falcon merchant.

"His house has been cleared out," he announced, oblivious to the tension that was in the room when he entered. "It looks like he ran as soon as Syfka found out who he was." Belatedly, he looked around. "Is there a problem?"

The serpent who had challenged us shook his head. "Just me, being . . . me." To Danica, he explained, "I shouldn't have spoken as I did. But I think I'm not the only one who still holds a little natural distrust of an avian soldier. Add to that learning they were falcons to begin with..." He shrugged. "My nest leader, my Diente and my Naga all speak for Kel and Andreios. That's enough. It's not as if I know anything helpful to you anyway; it's none of my business."

Once again A'isha took charge, though this time she did so in a decidedly cooled atmosphere. "The dancer's guilds are as old as Maeve's coven. Any obscure information we have about falcons and falcon laws would be in the texts downstairs. Even if we can't find a way to bring our dancers home, we may find something helpful for the future."

As nice as that sounded, it was less helpful than one would imagine. Of the writings done by the ancient coven, all that was left were copies of copies of words written in the old language, and much of them were obscured by mythical fancies.

The sun set over the nest, and dancers around the room stood and stretched, arching their bodies as the red light trickled into the room from the open ceiling. A pair went around the room and lit lamps, then stroked the embers of the previous night's fire into full bloom again.

Danica lay beside me as I pored over one of the many inscriptions, tired eyes befuddled by the whirling designs the letters formed.

"Well, I feel useless," Danica sighed.

"I'm not doing much better," I admitted. "I studied the old language when I was younger—every cobra does—but only enough to have the barest understanding. All this is written using more complex forms, and many of the symbols seem to have been either embellished or abbreviated. *This* squiggle, for instance, is completely meaningless to me."

Valene shifted to peer over my shoulder. *"Lar,"* she translated. "I think. *She'maen'ne'lar.* Or—wait, I see it. Someone copied the breaks wrong. *She'maen'nelar.*"

Danica rolled onto her back, running her hands through her hair as she yawned. "Valene, I'm suddenly even more impressed with you than I ever was."

The raven smiled at the compliment. "On Ahnmik, it's traditional to fill the space around letters with further designs that complement the lines of the writing. I think a few of these were copied from writings like that, which means it's very likely mistakes were made. I've been reading one where half the marks don't resemble any symbol I've ever seen in my life."

"I found a description of Queen Alasdair," A'isha called. "Whoever copied it made a note that the first draft was attributed to Kiesha."

Danica brightened, moving over to where A'isha was reading. "What does it say?"

"Mana'o'saerre'la'Alasdair . . . the hawk queen, Alasdair . . . *rai'maen'ferat'jaes'girian* . . . golden lady . . . hmm . . . Valene?"

The raven took over, skimming the piece a few times before she read it slowly. "The hawk queen, Alasdair, is both a golden lady and a young girl, with too much power for her years. She is serene, but there is a sadness in her eyes I cannot speak to. She is the same age as my son, and I pity her for not ever sharing his freedom to be a child."

The words were bittersweet, and familiar to us all. Everyone born during war knew what it was to see childhood fade too quickly as pain and loss stole the years away.

"The serpiente were only in Alasdair's city for a single night," Danica said softly. "How could words like those have been written just hours before the avian-serpiente war began?"

I shook my head. We would probably never know what really happened that night, or why. We would only ever know the aftermath, and hope we could reach past it.

CHAPTER 18

"ZANE! DANICA!"

I groggily lifted my head as I heard A'isha's and Valene's excited cries. Danica did the same beside me, blinking sleepily as we were both awoken. Judging by the otherwise silent nest, it was probably barely before dawn.

A'isha brushed aside the bits of writing we had been working on when sleep had taken us, and she tumbled to sit in front of us.

"I kept thinking last night that Rei was my student, one of my dancers, and so I should be able to protect him. Like I said yesterday, the guild has *always* dealt with its own. Nest justice *always* comes before outside rule. With very few exceptions, even the Cobriana have acknowledged that."

I found myself wondering whether she ever slept, as my own sleep-deprived brain fought to catch up with her thoughts. "Unfortunately, serpiente tradition won't stay a falcon's hand," I said.

"That's what I first thought, too," A'isha answered. "Valene thinks otherwise."

The raven's voice was excited despite her obvious fatigue. "The dancer's guild originated with the *Nesera'rsh*, a powerful group from the time of Maeve's coven. From what I can tell, they're the modern equivalent among Anhamirak's followers of the falcons' Mercy. I didn't think much of it until A'isha found this." Valene began to read the flowing, slippery words of the old language excitedly.

"Maeve'hena'o'Dasi'mana-La'pt'hena'o'itilfera'alistair . . ."

Danica and I both blinked at the incomprehensible language. Valene translated swiftly. " 'Maeve stands as leader to our thirteen, and we as guides and guardians to the village. We speak our rituals to the realm of the divine, but it is the Rsh who hold the records, and speak law and justice to the land. Each'—the closest translation I can think of is *nest*—'is a realm unto itself, and *its rule over its own is undisputed even by our voice.*' "

I stared at the page, desperately wondering if what I thought was true.

Valene confirmed my suspicions. "The original was written by one of the thirteen members of Maeve's coven. Specifically, by the hand of shm'Ahnmik'la'Cjarsa—the falcon Empress. Kel could be a trickier case, but Andreios was studying with A'isha. Cjarsa herself acknowledged the independent law of the *Nesera'rsh*, and in current day, that means this guild."

Their excitement was infectious, but I struggled to stay reasonable. "These words were written thousands of years ago. Much as I would like to believe them, it seems unlikely that the falcons will relinquish Araceli's only child because we discovered words that were written before the Dasi split."

Valene listened to my doubts, but spoke calmly once I was done. "There's a line in the old myths about how

'Ahnmik turns all vows true, all lies apparent, and the written word as blood in stone.' It would seem reasonable that some of that would carry over into their magic. I would have mentioned it earlier, but I never imagined we would find proof of any vow we could possibly hold the falcons *to*."

Still, I found it hard to believe that these powerful creatures could be so easily manipulated by ancient texts. "You sound more certain than I would be, if I had only that one line of myth to go on." I tried to make my voice gentle, because I did not want to destroy what was so far our only hope, but I also could not let them charge into a plan with no basis in fact.

"I've seen for myself how a falcon treats promises as irrevocably binding, whether she wishes to or not. . . ." Valene took a breath and continued, "Erica was thirteen and Kel sixteen when Kel first came to us. The night Erica's brother died, Kel held the girl and told her, 'The sun will rise tomorrow, and life will go on. It will still hurt. You will still miss him. But eventually things will get better.' Erica asked her, 'You promise?' "

Valene shook her head. "Kel just turned away, and I was furious. She told me later that she couldn't make that promise, because we were in the middle of a war. We could all be killed, and even if we weren't, she wasn't sure things *would* get better. I told her Erica needed hope. I asked her, 'Would it have killed you to make that promise?' She looked away from me and said, 'Maybe.' "

The raven's lip began to quiver. A'isha went to her and held her hand as she drew several deep breaths.

A'isha spoke while Valene composed herself. "If it's true that Ahnmik's magic forbids even that kind of white lie, then maybe it really would hold Cjarsa to these laws. No matter how long ago she wrote them, she signed her name and made them her vow."

Something else occurred to me as A'isha spoke. "When you gave the *Ahnleh* to Danica, you said the charms used to be worn by the *Nesera'rsh*. You thought there was a time when even enemies at war wouldn't harm someone who wore one." A'isha nodded, and I turned to Danica. "None of us could have stopped Araceli from threatening you at the Keep, but after she saw the pendant, she backed off."

Danica nodded. "It seemed like a miracle at the time, but maybe . . ."

"If our charm could stay a falcon's hand, then the word of the descendants of the *Nesera'rsh* could be enough to bring one of our own home. It's still a long shot," A'isha said, though her voice was light with excitement. "It would require the royal house first listening to our petition, and then acknowledging Rei as one of ours—which I imagine they'll be reluctant to do if it means they will lose him. But it seems the best chance we have."

Valene had recovered enough to add, "I can speak for us, as a dancer and a raven, so they can't deny Rei's place in the nest because of his feathers. As for Kel—" Again she hesitated. "You said Syfka would have pardoned her?"

"She was willing to leave her with us," Danica replied. "She believes exile in our lands would be as great a punishment as any the Empress would level."

Valene nodded. "I understand Kel was once a favorite of the Empress. If Cjarsa was willing to release her once, perhaps she will allow Syfka's sentence to stand."

The hope still hung on magics we did not understand, but it was better than none at all, and every moment made it seem more possible.

"Valene, you are willing to do this?" I asked. Though Valene had not spoken of any danger posed to the messenger, I did not count on benevolence from any creature who would carry away our loyal guards and hold a blade to my queen's throat.

"I am the only dancer you have who is capable of flying to Ahnmik," she pointed out. "Further, no one in this nest is as fluent in their language or as versed in the etiquette of falcon society. I *have* to do this—for Rei, and for Kel."

"Very well, then. When do you wish to leave?"

"As soon as possible. It will take me a few days to get there, and I do not know how long I will need to wait before I am allowed an audience."

"I have one question before you go." Danica's eyes were focused on the paper the dancers had found. "Valene, would you read this line again?"

"La'pt'hena'o'itilfera'alistair," the raven answered.

"That's the line about guides and guardians?" Danica asked.

A'isha finally made the connection Danica had as her finger hovered over the letters. "Yes. This word is alistair."

"And this?" Now Danica pointed to a series of symbols at the bottom of the page.

Valene answered, *"A'le-Ahnleh.* It is a blessing, and means, more or less, *by the will of fate.* Ahnleh is hardly legible anymore on the ancient coins, but it is the Snakecharm on your pendant, from the nest. Among the serpiente, it is used at the bottom of many documents, as a mark of promise, truth. As you can see, it's also nearly identical to the Seal of Alasdair, which has always been used on binding works among the avians." Her joking tone poorly masked a certain resentment as she warned, "Though be careful not to point it out to the Tuuli Thea. The last one exiled me from the courts for daring to point out the similarity."

Danica smiled slightly, lifting her gaze from the page. "I will be sure not to let her know. Is it coincidence?" she asked.

Valene shrugged. "Your mother wanted it to be. I prefer to think that our records are wrong—that, before the wars, perhaps Kiesha's and Alasdair's people lived together peacefully. Something went horribly wrong somewhere, but before that, there must have been a time when the serpiente and avians were close enough for words and ideas like *Ahnleh* and *alistair* to become shared."

"Our history books say that the word 'alistair' is a variation of Alasdair, as she was the first true protector of her people. Perhaps it was the other way around, and she was named protector from this word," Danica theorized.

The glow was back in her face, and she was not hiding her excitement.

Abruptly, she turned and kissed me. "Zane, if this is true..." She trailed off, her golden eyes so wide and bright that I drew her closer to me. "Can you imagine what kind of world it might have been?"

I tried to picture a time when avians and serpiente lived side by side. Not as they did in this wary peace we held, in which intrepid scholars and merchants sometimes dared to visit the other side, but coexisting in one land where they weren't afraid of each other.

I wondered if re-creating that world was possible.

It seemed like such an incredible idea, but I couldn't help entertaining it. "We were worried that our child would need to be either avian or serpiente, because the two lands she would rule would be separated that way. What if we could let her be both, and give her a world that is blended just as surely as her blood will be?"

A'isha asked, "Just build somewhere that isn't Keep or palace, but both?"

"Why not?" Danica asked. "A'isha, your nest has serpents, falcons, ravens and hawks sharing it now. If that is possible, then how impossible could it be to re-create a world where they don't just dance together, but live together? We're stymied now because people are afraid to immerse themselves in another world, leaving the Keep for the serpiente market or the other way around, but a third court wouldn't be specifically one or the other. We could design the court so it's only a small step from home to . . . to a land where a queen can be both cobra and hawk, because her people are just as mixed."

A'isha paused, contemplating, and we all waited for her response. If she refused, then this hope was all but lost. The dancers were among the most tolerant of my kind; if their leader could not imagine that this place Danica and I had suddenly invented was possible, then no one else would.

"I would join a dragon's nest," A'isha affirmed finally. "If only for the challenge."

"Dragon?" I asked.

"A dragon is a winged serpent, isn't it?" A'isha replied.

"I've always thought of them as winged lizards, though I've never seen one myself."

"A wyvern, then," A'isha corrected. "Wyvern's Nest. Perhaps some of your avian scholars could share their myths and stories for a *she'da;* I should like to create such a dance someday, maybe one that will rival the famous Namir-da." She frowned, adding seriously, "Though it would have to be very subtle to be acceptable to an avian audience."

"Do you think the rest of your nest would be willing?" I asked.

"Honestly? Not all." She shrugged. "But you do not need all; you need only a few, who have the courage to try to show our beliefs to a feathered audience so they can understand and perhaps join us. Give us a nest, give us a fire and the audience that would come with your new land, and we will be honored to dance for a Wyvern's Court. Sha'Mehay has become too small, anyway."

I continued pondering. "Merchants would come if there was a market for them. If we dedicated some land for schooling, we could bring in the scholars of both our courts—who, hopefully, would be willing to try to learn from each other."

Danica echoed my thoughts from her own perspective. "The avian court follows the Tuuli Thea. They would be hesitant to bring their families so close to the serpiente, at least at first, but hopefully future generations won't be as frightened. And if we let it be known that we will raise our child there, I think that plenty of avian scholars would be willing to go, if only in hopes of 'protecting' the queen's heir. Then of course there may be those who simply wish to curry favor with their monarch, even if it means supporting what they will doubtless see as another mad scheme by their Tuuli Thea."

"Another?"

"Of course," she answered sweetly. "You may recall the last one, since it involved announcing you as my alistair."

CHAPTER 19

O UR ANIMATED CHATTER awakened the rest of the nest, most of whom took it as a cue to rise and begin their rituals to greet the day. Danica and I were each drawn into the simple, slow-moving dances. As soon as those morning dances were done, Valene left for Ahnmik. We watched her take to the skies, the rising sun on her heels, as powerful black wings carried her into the west.

Afterward, Danica and I sought breakfast in the market. It was a slightly more peaceful place to pause and contemplate the ideas the night had brought us.

"It seems like such an incredible plan, I find myself wondering if it is even possible, and struggling to conceive of how to begin such a project," said Danica. Testing the sounds for not the first time, she sighed, "Wyvern's Court."

"We'll need to speak to Irene, and your mother," I asserted. "If either one of them rejects this idea, there is no way we will succeed. Any potential heirs to either throne—hawk or cobra—must be raised in the same mixed-blood land, or people will feel they can still choose to be apart."

Danica nodded, so I continued.

"Then I suppose we seek the approval of our respective courts, and allow the information into the markets. Once we are sure we have support, we can consult with architects, artists, whoever we need to try to bring this place we are imagining to life."

After that, we ate breakfast in silence, sifting through our thoughts like children going through colored stones—optimistic, because although some were too dark and some were too sharp, many glittered like precious gems.

"I have an excuse to be up at this mad hour." Irene yawned as we located her in Salem's nursery. "Why are you looking so bright-eyed?"

As she spoke, she rocked Salem in her arms. The babe kept shifting from boy to cobra, trying to wriggle out of her grip, then turning back to human form to pout when she wouldn't let him.

"We're plotting reformation of life as we know it," I replied, somewhat flippantly.

"Oh, is that all?" she teased. "Why not start with breakfast?"

"Thank you, but no," I answered. "Danica and I actually wanted your feedback on an idea we had."

Quickly, we detailed the conception of Wyvern's Court, from finding the two symbols to getting A'isha's support. Irene listened quietly, nodding every now and then as she finally managed to settle Salem down.

When we paused for her response, she looked hopefully at the face of her child. "If you can create such a place," she finally answered, "I would be honored to raise my son there.

And I have never seen you two fail to achieve any dream you strive toward."

We arrived at the Hawk's Keep the next evening. Nacola greeted us the moment we stepped into the courtyard, with Gerard by her side.

"I hope this unexpected visit doesn't mean that there is a problem," Nacola said firmly.

"Nothing is wrong," Danica assured her as we walked past the first-floor market to a private parlor on the second floor. "Zane and I simply wanted to speak to you about an idea we had."

"For Rei—" Gerard cut off abruptly, as if deciding it wasn't his place to question us, no matter how much he must have wanted to know about his former flight members.

"The dancers found something we hope we can use to force Cjarsa's hand, at least regarding Andreios," I said. "Actually, Valene Silvermead was the one who made that discovery. She has gone to Ahnmik to petition the falcon Empress for his return."

"Thank you, sir."

After Danica shut the door, I broached the reason for our visit.

"While we were looking for something to use against the falcons, we found something else—something that might be even more pertinent to our current situation."

Danica and I went on to explain her discoveries in the texts, and Valene's theories regarding a possible history together. Then we described our new dream.

When we were done, Nacola drew a deep breath and said, "It seems I do owe Valene an apology. She has obviously done much for these lands in the time since she left my court—though I am not sure whether I agree with it all."

Nacola sighed. "Your dreams are vast, Danica, but they include as many obstacles as rewards."

She went on to list all the problems with a Wyvern's Court. "People from both groups will be hesitant to bring their children to a place such as Wyvern's Court. You may create one generation, but for such a place to prosper, you need families. And I can think of many reasons any avian mother would pale at the thought of her daughter being surrounded by dancers and—" She cut off, then continued, "And serpiente pastimes our people long ago deemed inappropriate for young children. Zane, I believe your people have an equally unflattering view of how we raise our children," she shot at me.

"Beyond the question of how to bring up children, you face the problem of now needing to juggle three lands, trying to shift power from the old two to the new one without forcing the destruction of the originals—which I assume is not your intent, as it would ruin the homes and livelihoods of many who live and work in those places.

"Finally, you are still faced with the problem of whether your child will, in the future, have an avian pair bond or a serpiente mate."

"We are hoping," I interrupted, trying to stop her tirade, "that by the time our child chooses her mate, whether he is scaled or feathered will not matter."

Nacola frowned, but before she could object, Danica spoke. "And she *will* choose her own partner. I chose my alistair, as you have now, too, Mother. If the next queen is raised as a member of both societies, to be Tuuli Thea and Diente both, then any man who wishes to court her will need to accept and love both sides of her—especially if he wishes to rule beside her."

Nacola countered, "You will still have trouble with families. I am certain you have realized that if all the Shardae and Cobriana children are raised well in the new land, it will encourage other parents to trust your Wyvern's Court. If any royal parent refuses, it will cause doubt among your people. I assume that is why you are speaking to me: You wish to know what I would choose, should I be lucky enough to bear another child. The answer . . ."

She paused, contemplative. "I may never have that joy," she finally said. "That means that you, Danica, are the only child I need to protect at this moment. I have seen you flourish these last several months, despite my objections and my hesitation. Should I have another child, I will raise her to be loyal to her Tuuli Thea, and her Tuuli Thea's heir. If that means raising her in a land where serpents and avians dwell side by side, then I imagine I will do what I must to support your efforts.

"However," she added swiftly, before either of us could speak, "I will make no promises as to the future until I see this dream made real."

"It is too late to gather our people this evening, and we are anxious to return to serpiente lands at first light," Danica said. "If you would speak to the court for us, showing your support, it would mean so much."

Nacola nodded. "I will present your Wyvern's Court, with all my blessings. Fly with grace."

CHAPTER 20

WHEN WE RETURNED TO SERPIENTE LANDS the next morning, we found a debate raging in the market. A group of serpents had gathered around a stall I knew belonged to an avian artist, completely obscuring her from our view. In the midst of all our hope, the raised voices chilled me.

"This is exactly why I didn't want to do this here!" A'isha's voice rose above the others. "Back up, back up!"

With Danica on one side and me on the other, we quickly formed a path through the crowd, to reveal a blushing artist with a stripe of gold paint on her cheek.

"I didn't mean for my little sketch to create such a stir," she said quietly, before I could ask what was going on. "I heard the rumors about a Wyvern's Court . . . and my imagination got the better of me."

"Show him," A'isha encouraged, because the artist was still standing protectively in front of her creation.

"It isn't finished," the woman said as she stepped shyly out of the way.

The background had only barely been sketched—a blue sky, and what looked to be the beginning of a market. But in the middle of the white slate plaza was a green marble mosaic. The design formed was similar to *Ahnleh*, but subtly different; the artist had overlapped the serpiente *Ahnleh* with the avian Seal of Alasdair. The two symbols were so similar that they fit together as if first designed as a single glyph, reformed here after more than two thousand years.

At the center of the symbol was a young woman in the midst of shifting shape; from her back grew golden wings, but her body was sliding into a serpent's form, and her head was thrown back so that her face was bathed in sunlight.

Wyvern.

Even with rough details, the image took my breath away.

"The dancers say that you and your mate hope to form a combined court," the artist said. "I heard the story of where the idea came from, and I could just . . . see it. I wanted to create it."

"So do we," Danica whispered.

Her quiet reply, confirming the rumors, brought a barrage of questions. Several minutes passed before I could quiet the crowd enough for me to speak.

"Apparently you have already heard about Wyvern's Court." I had not expected our dream to stay a secret for long. Few things did once the dancers knew of them. "It's true. We intend to create a place where avians and serpents live together. Nacola Shardae has given her blessing and is speaking to the avian court on our behalf. Irene Cobriana has also agreed, as has the leader of sha'Mehay. I hope you will, too."

Again, the simple words brought a storm of replies, so much that eventually A'isha invited us, along with the avian artist, back to the nest, where we could think without being questioned. Before we had reached sha'Mehay, however, we were approached by a young raven I knew as Tadeo.

"My Tuuli Thea, Diente . . . I heard A'isha speaking to my father—he's a weaver?" he offered hopefully.

"I know your father," I answered, which made the raven blush like an adolescent corn snake. "He was one of the first avian merchants in our market."

Danica paused, and then exclaimed, "Of course! Tadeo. The last I heard, you were in the midst of another apprenticeship."

"Mm." The raven ducked his head for a moment. "Yes, milady. I've . . . had some false starts."

That was an understatement. From what I'd been told, in the past three years, Tadeo had shifted his apprenticeship from the study of music, to philosophy, to history, to architecture and now to art.

Tadeo continued without encouragement. "The artist I've been working with most recently—well, before my father called me home—lives beside a small lake, about half a day's flight from here. There's an area nearby where the land sinks, forming a valley with hills on three sides and a cliff on the fourth."

"I know where you're talking about," I answered. The valley was a beautiful area, with granite too close to the surface to allow for the deep-rooted trees of the surrounding forest, and wildflowers everywhere.

"I was thinking of it, especially when I saw that painting. It's about the same distance from the Keep and this market, just a little farther east. It's on the edge of the land claimed by a pack of wolf shapeshifters, but they don't hunt in that area, and according to my teacher, they have started to express interest in trading with us since the war ended. . . ." He looked at us hopefully.

"Why don't you come inside with us?" Danica suggested. "You can tell us more."

I looked at A'isha, expecting her to protest our inviting more avians from the Keep to her nest, but she just nodded. "This seems as good a place as any to confer—plenty of room to work, and rooms downstairs for anyone who is traveling and does not feel like sleeping in the main room like a dancer."

"In that case," I suggested, "we should see about bringing in other artists and architects who are interested in helping, and inviting some others from the Keep. I know the area Tadeo is describing. If he is correct that the wolves would not object, then I agree it might be the perfect place to create Wyvern's Court." Tadeo blushed again at those words.

"Pardon me, but I am well acquainted with both the court and the market," someone said. I turned to see Fisk Falchion, another avian merchant, behind us. "If you would like, I would be honored to fly to the Keep for you and see who would be interested in coming to work with us here."

I did not relish the thought of yet another long ride on horseback, so I accepted the offer immediately, as did Danica. Fisk took to the skies, promising to bring back the best artists and architects he knew, as well as some teachers and merchants whose ideas might prove useful in the creation of the markets and schools.

Our remaining two avian guests entered sha'Mehay as if they were stepping into a temple, their eyes wide as they took in the studying dancers. A'isha, Danica and I discussed which of the serpiente we should invite, and as the afternoon lengthened, the crowd around the fire grew.

Oddly enough, it was Tadeo who shone the most, taking the role of organizer. By the time Fisk returned with a group of avians, Tadeo had already set people into groups, each working on a different part of the new land.

The merchants were put together to discuss how the market would be designed. Avian and serpiente scholars sat down together warily, but with some encouragement, they began to debate how best to combine their skills. A'isha led a group in designing Wyvern's Nest, and in choosing who would be allowed to travel to the new nest to found it. Artists and architects claimed by far the largest area, as they created sketch after sketch, trying to blend the two distinctly different styles.

The day turned to night, as it was wont to do even among the most inspired. The nest quieted, a few dancers performing their last stretches and prayers of thanks before they curled up around the fire. Most of the avian consultants left for their own homes and beds, but a few—Tadeo included—collapsed where they had been working, sleeping in the nest as the dancers did.

I saw one serpent lie down not far from where the raven was curled up asleep. She drew a blanket over them both and snuggled against his back.

Amazing how far we had come. A few days ago, I had been surprised to see Rei and Valene accepted as dancers in the nest; now anyone who wanted a part in this project was welcome. We had achieved half the goal of Wyvern's Court simply by dreaming of it.

CHAPTER 21

OVER THE COURSE OF THE NEXT FORTNIGHT, the dream flourished. Soon one could hardly walk across sha'Mehay without dodging notes, charts, lists, diagrams or designs.

Tadeo continued as the leader, working with his previous teacher to measure out the valley and mark the locations of pathways, houses, shops, the market center and a three-story structure built into the northern cliffs that would serve the same purpose as the Hawk's Keep and the serpiente palace.

Pointing to his sketched map of the area, Tadeo explained, "The brook and pool don't have the best drinking water, but there are three springs in the cliffs that are cold and fresh. One is higher up—a couple of sparrows found it. It's about the right height for us to build a fountain around it, and have it central in the top story of the Keep—or palace, or whatever you want to call it. The building is going to be worked into the side of the cliff. In the end it will stand tall and grand, but still be rooted deeply in the earth—a perfect combination of avian and serpiente ideals."

He continued his updates, which he had given us every evening since the project had begun.

Danica and I both turned at a shocked cry from Lincon, one of the avian merchants from the Keep. "Not in the middle of the market!" He looked horrified by whatever his serpiente companion had said.

"Where else would you put them?" the serpent replied, sounding genuinely puzzled.

"I thought A'isha was dealing with your dancers," the avian said, gesturing vaguely toward A'isha and her group.

"They *are* designing the nest, but there needs to be somewhere for them to perform."

Fisk joined the discussion. "The dancers are a crucial part of serpiente culture, not to mention a beautiful addition to any public area."

"They may be important to the serpiente, but making their performances so accessible to our children just isn't appropriate," Lincon said. "Wouldn't it make more sense for the dancers to remain in their nest, so the more impressionable of our ..." He trailed off, because the room had suddenly gone very quiet around him.

A'isha flitted over to the avian man, wrapped in quiet anger. "Have we harmed you in some way while you have been here? Has one of my dancers offended you?"

Lincon pointed out, "It is not your hospitality I question, but your regard for propriety. I was propositioned within moments of entering your nest."

A'isha chuckled, shaking her head. "You are a pretty man, and you walked in alone."

Lincon cleared his throat. "I don't think this is a laughing matter. Our young men and women should not be exposed to such—"

I stepped between the two before the argument could go further. "Wyvern's Court is not going to be a place where avians and serpents can turn their backs on each other, like neighbors who never speak. Our artists can't be the only ones here who are willing to compromise. Every teacher, parent, child and merchant will need to do the same. A'isha, that may mean teaching your dancers to exercise care around avians new to Wyvern's Court." To Lincon, I added, "Compromise may also mean letting unattached ladies and gentlemen make their own decisions and mistakes."

I looked at Danica, remembering the first uneasy months after she had agreed to become my mate. She smiled encouragingly.

"We come from different worlds," I said, "but each has so much to teach the other. There will be moments of dissonance, when people struggle to understand each other's ways, but once we get past our misconceptions, imagine the reward.

"The dancers *will* perform in the market of Wyvern's Court; they will be beside avian poets, singers, philosophers and storytellers or we cannot hope to succeed. Merchants will haggle prices and barter goods as they have in both our markets throughout history. Scholars will work to impart their valuable knowledge to their students. Artists will create beauty. And our children will grow up together, playing the same games, taught by the same teachers, *living* side by side until as adults, I pray, they laugh at the petty arguments we had in this nest while we designed their world."

"And ravens will dance, and serpents will fight for the lives of falcons." The soft voice drew our attention to the doorway of the nest.

Valene swayed by the door, her face pale and shining with sweat.

"Valene, are you all right?" Danica darted past me to take Valene's arm and lead her inside.

The raven nodded. "It is . . . a long flight. I just need to rest." Despite her obvious exhaustion, she said, "I spoke to Empress Cjarsa. She said she would consider my words; then she sent me home. . . . I don't know what she will do."

"Thank you."

"I heard you speaking when I came in," she said, lifting her head enough to look at me. She gestured to those surrounding us. "Is this a dream?"

"This is real," I assured her.

She smiled, but her eyes were heavy-lidded. "I thought I might have fallen asleep already."

"That might be a good idea," A'isha said. "You're shaking with exhaustion. Let me help you downstairs, so you can rest. You have done much for us."

Danica, A'isha and I helped the exhausted raven downstairs and saw her tucked securely into bed.

As we turned to leave, a serpent approached. Her expression held a bit of nervousness, as did her voice. "Zane, Danica, do you have a moment? I'd like to show you something."

A'isha returned to the main nest as we followed the new serpent to one of the other rooms downstairs. I spent the brief walk trying to place her face, which seemed familiar in one way, but completely alien in another.

She stopped in the empty hall before one of the bedroom doors. The illusion rippled away at the same time that she said, "Before you act, remember that it was not I who took your people. Nor was it I who sentenced Kel to death."

Danica and I both recoiled from Syfka as she shed the

magic that had hidden her. The falcon held out her hands, palms up in a timeless gesture of harmlessness—one that was an utter lie—and said before either of us could speak, "Your raven speaks the old language almost like a falcon, and she is as quick to twist ancient laws to her advantage as Empress Cjarsa herself."

"And what of her request?" Syfka's dark words about Kel made Danica's voice soft. Danica's hand again found mine, seeking support.

"Though Sebastian was well hidden, Kel does not have the power to veil herself from royal blood," Syfka explained. "I did everything I could to avoid bringing either of them home, and believe me, the Empress was not pleased with my failure."

"You did not seem so anxious to help us while you were here," Danica pointed out.

"I have no desire to *help* you or them," Syfka answered. "But a crow has no right to the royal house, and despite his birth, Sebastian is far too tainted by his life here to be called anything else. And despite Cjarsa's blind affection for the girl who was once hers, Kel will cause nothing but problems among our people. I would have gladly abandoned them both here, but Araceli was not anxious to give up her kin."

"So what now?" I demanded. "You would not be here if you—"

"Araceli ordered Kel executed," Syfka interrupted. "I convinced her that there were better ways to deal with the girl that would not martyr her. Eventually she concurred with my sentence."

"And Rei—Sebastian?"

"Sebastian is dead," she said. Danica's hand gripped

mine more tightly, until Syfka added, "In his mother's eyes, anyway. I give your Andreios to you, provided you assure me you will keep him."

"Give . . ." Danica's eyes widened.

"It was lucky that Valene spoke to me first, and I decided to take her to the Empress. Cjarsa honors such ancient laws, but Araceli might have been inclined to make your raven disappear. Fortunately for you, the heir still must answer to the Empress, no matter how disinclined she was to give up her only son." Syfka nodded at the room behind her. "Your people are there, somewhat worse for wear—and officially barred from our lands. Should they return, the raven dancer included, they will be executed on sight."

"Thank you," Danica managed to reply.

The falcon tossed her head. "Don't thank me. They both paid the price for their crimes. Though considering what I see here, they may soon regret your efforts to regain them. Snakes and birds," she spat. "It was never meant to be."

"Somehow, I don't find your opinion important," Danica replied. "Now step aside so I can see my people."

As I watched, Syfka's form again shifted to that of a familiar-seeming dancer. I had no doubt that she would walk out of the nest as easily unnoticed as she had come in. Danica rushed past me to the room where Rei and Kel were supposed to be.

Kel was kneeling as we entered, bending over Rei's still form.

She looked up as we came closer, and I winced at what I saw. Her violet eyes were dull with fatigue; only a hint of triumph in her gaze kept me from hating myself for not fighting more to keep her. The left side of her jaw was the sickly green-yellow color that a bad bruise turns before it heals.

Strands of hair had fallen out of her ponytail and hung around her face.

She was wearing a falcon shirt, which left her arms and most of her back bare, and the skin it revealed had livid welts, bruises and deep cuts that had yet to fully close. Her shoulders glistened with what looked like faint silver lines drawn across her skin to form symbols that were both familiar and strange.

Rei was resting in Kel's arms, unconscious but breathing. His face was shadowed by his nearly black hair, but like Kel's, the skin I could see was bruised, cut or shimmering with what I suspected was some strange falcon magic.

"You're truly with us?" Danica whispered. "Syfka said . . . I barely believed her." Danica fell to her knees beside the pair, reaching forward and then pulling her hands back as if afraid she would hurt them. "You need a doctor."

Kel shook her head sharply. "I'll heal. Some of these will scar, but . . . they're meant to. No doctor will keep my skin from being marked when Araceli went out of her way to make it so. Rei will be fine, too. He passed out barely after we touched the ground here; please let him sleep."

Kel lifted Rei, gently laying him on the bed before she begged of us, "Please, water?"

"Of course," Danica answered, standing quickly. "I'll bring it. Rei can rest here, and you are welcome to use one of the other rooms. Do you want anything to eat, or should we let you sleep?"

The falcon hesitated. "Food. I don't think I've eaten . . . in a very long time. Thank you, milady. . . . Danica, my true queen."

CHAPTER 22

KEL INSISTED ON GOING UPSTAIRS into the nest instead of staying downstairs, where it was calmer.

"I need to prove to myself I really am back here," she explained softly as A'isha chastised the people who had immediately descended with questions. "The nest is so infinitely different from the white city."

She broke off the instant food was presented to her, staring at it for long moments as if not believing her eyes. After that, she ate with a hunger that reminded me more of wolves than of graceful falcons.

She also drained glass after glass of water and finally slowed enough to sip a hot tea. The color began to return to her skin, though in places the change served only to accentuate her injuries.

"Feathered Hades, girl, when did you last *eat*?" Tadeo gawked. He was almost hustled out of the nest, but Kel smiled wearily.

"Before I left the Keep," she answered. Her voice was as

dry as dust, and she took another sip of her tea, which was flavored generously with honey and sage.

"It's been weeks," I protested. She was obviously thinner, but not so much—

Kel managed an expression too tired to be patronizing, then answered simply, "When I was four years old, I stood in the Ahnmik courtyard for a fortnight, not moving, drinking or eating, just focusing on my magic. The test is one all falcon children take, to see whether they have the power to be—oh, but you don't care; it doesn't matter now. That world is gone to me and good riddance."

With these last words, she emptied her tea and sat back in her chair, closing her eyes.

"How good it is to be here," she sighed.

A small sound brought our attention to where a much-bedraggled Andreios stood in the doorway. He was gripping the edge of the frame, but his eyes took in everything around him, as if he was as starved for the warmth and companionship of the nest as Kel was for food.

I offered him my hand, too grateful to have him back to speak.

Rei looked at it for a moment as if not understanding, then gripped it as if he would lose the earth if he let it go. Leaning on me, he made it with near-grace to the fireside.

As Kel had, Rei put away more food than I had ever seen him eat in one sitting, and he drained water glasses as fast as they were set before him. Every now and then he would stop, his eyes lifting and lingering on something with disbelief— sometimes Danica, sometimes me and quite often Kel.

Only after the food was gone did he ask Kel, "You came after me?"

She nodded.

"I'm sorry," he whispered.

"Don't be." Her voice was also soft, but it held no uncertainty. "You are needed here."

"My mother was not happy to part with me."

"No," Kel answered, "she wasn't."

For a while, there was no conversation, as no one wanted to be the first to question the falcons about what had happened, and everyone wrestled with curiosity.

Finally, Danica raised her voice in one word to Andreios: "How?"

I knew she wasn't only asking how he had gotten out. Rei started at the beginning, the part Danica was most curious about.

"We were together in the Keep's library when you heard that Andreios was gone. Remember I tried to stop you from going after him," he answered, voice pained. "I followed you, to keep you safe, but I was too slow. One of the serpiente struck you across the head. Another bit your Andreios. I fought them off, but you were unconscious and Andreios was poisoned. I tried to force-change him, but . . ." We already knew the result. "It was too late, or I wasn't strong enough. I had just enough energy to bring you home, and then I collapsed. I had taken too much of the poison from Rei trying to save him; it nearly killed me. It was days before I was fully awake, and then I was locked in Andreios's form for days before I regained my strength."

He took a deep sip of his water, looking at Kel to continue for him.

"He had already disobeyed a direct order to return, insisting instead that he wanted to swear his loyalty to a different queen. For most falcons, that would have been enough to merit death. No one would dare execute Araceli's only child, even for treason, but then he stole a crow's form," she explained. "It is one thing for a guard to acquire another form in the service of her Empress, as sometimes happens, but quite another to sully the royal house. It took them years to come searching for him because it took Araceli that long to convince the Empress that he should still be considered a falcon, and not put to death as a mongrel."

"I knew I could not go home," Rei continued, "and I was terrified that you would force me away if I told you what had happened." Finally he raised his eyes to Danica, his expression pleading. "I swore my life and my loyalty to you, to protect you no matter the cost, no matter the situation. I stayed as Andreios first because I was frightened not to be him, but later because he gave me an identity. I could not save him, but he could save me."

Danica brushed her fingertips across his cheek. "You are Rei. To me, you will always be Rei." She shook her head. "I understand. I forgive you."

"Thank you, Dani."

Danica smiled at the nickname, but then the expression faded as I asked, "What now?"

Defiantly, Kel asserted, "They hold no claim to either of us now. Our magic is bound. Our falcon forms are bound. I have my sparrow and Rei has his crow, and we have the forms you see now, but that is all."

"Just mortals now," Rei whispered. He watched Kel as he explained, "The Empress had her Mercy take from Kel what she had learned that threatened the island."

Kel briefly touched a mark on her left wrist, which I had not noticed since she had returned to her true form. I did not recognize the symbol. "The Mercy works in pairs; if one strays, her partner reprimands her. The Empress broke the bond, and she took the memories..." She paused, then finished, "to protect Ahnmik, and to protect... I don't know." She dropped her head, leaning it on her hands for a moment. "I don't know. 'Just mortals now.' "

Rei stood and wrapped his arms around her. "Thank the sky, just mortals now."

Kel laughed a little, but it was bitter laughter. I suspected the memories behind it would only give me reason to shudder in the dark as I imagined what these two loyal souls had endured, together.

"A finer mortal I've never known," she replied. She turned to Danica and asked with a rhetorical, detached air, "I suppose my stint as leader of the Royal Flight was very short-lived?"

Rei shook his head. "Take the position."

"Either way, I won't have it long," Kel replied. "I'd like to ask milady's permission to court an alistair."

Danica raised one brow, and I could not help smiling at Rei's shocked expression.

"That's not exactly the way it's usually done," Danica answered, though her tone was light enough to say she would not deny the request.

"Commonly, I believe an alistair courts a lady, but I'm tired of waiting for him to pick up on my hints," Kel said.

Rei still looked a little scandalized.

"Of course, Kel," Danica answered, squeezing my hand. "Though the Royal Flight will miss you and your alistair."

Kel immediately turned to Rei, teasing, "I believe I can only have a falcon for my alistair, and since you're the only falcon present—"

"No," Rei interrupted, shaking his head. "This isn't right

at all. An alistair is sworn to defend his pair bond, to protect her with his life."

Are you willing to swear upon your own spirit and the sky above that you will protect Danica Shardae from all harm? I recalled vividly the day Andreios had asked me that, in front of the avian court, as the first of the vows sworn by an alistair.

Without hesitation I answered that question again in my mind:

I swear it.

I wondered now only why Rei would not, when it was obvious that these two souls were perfect for each other.

"Is that a problem?" Kel asked, her voice suddenly sounding a little more fragile than before.

"It is when *you* came after *me*. So long as we're altering tradition, I do believe I should be asking you, Kel, to be my alistair."

Kel paused for a moment. "Faultless logic. With milady and my lord's permission," she said, glancing at Danica and me to receive our nods of encouragement, "I accept."

Kel leaned over to kiss her pair bond. I spun Danica to her feet, leading her in a few steps of the Namir-da before simply holding her close. Someone behind us in the nest cheered, and others picked up the cry—avian, serpiente, falcon, scaled or feathered, for tonight the differences didn't matter.

In the temple of Anhamirak, the steps were different each day and each eve, but each dance was still one. They danced the only dance, the one Anhamirak weaves.

Hope, trust, love, life.
Sha'Ahnleh: They danced with Fate.

Amelia Atwater-Rhodes grew up in Concord, Massachusetts. Born in 1984, she wrote her first novel, *In the Forests of the Night*, praised as "remarkable" *(Voice of Youth Advocates)* and "mature and polished" *(Booklist)*, when she was thirteen. She has since published *Demon in My View, Shattered Mirror*, and *Midnight Predator*, all ALA Quick Picks for Young Adults, and *Hawksong*, a *School Library Journal* Best Book of the Year and a *Voice of Youth Advocates* Best Science Fiction, Fantasy, and Horror selection.

Lebanon Valley College
Bishop Library
Annville, PA 17003

GAYLORD RG